James Hogg (1770–1835), was born on his father's farm in the Ettrick Forest near Selkirk in the Scottish Borders. He left school for farm work at the age of seven and became a shepherd in his teens. Steeped in the oral tradition and encouraged by one of his employers, he determined to be a poet like Burns. He became friends with Walter Scott when the latter's interest in collecting old ballads led him to Hogg's mother. Hogg's various ventures into farming did not succeed. In 1810 he went to Edinburgh to seek a literary career. Success finally came in 1813 with *The Queen's Wake*. In his *Poetic Mirror* (1816), Hogg satirised Wordsworth, Byron, Scott and other contemporary poets.

Hogg's first novels *The Brownie of Bodsbeck* (1818) and *The Three Perils of Man* (1822), drew on the folk tradition, but they also have a unique imaginative energy which was never fully appreciated or understood by the more genteel arbiters of taste in Edinburgh. *The Three Perils of Woman* (1823) was not well received and *The Private Memoirs and Confessions of a Justified Sinner* made equally little impact when it first appeared (anonymously) in 1824.

Hogg continued to publish poetry, with *Queen Hynde* (1825) and *Songs, by the Ettrick Shepherd* (1831), and was even more prolific in prose, with *Altrive Tales* in 1832, and a controversial memoir of the late Sir Walter Scott in 1834. Still more stories, *Tales of the Wars of Montrose*, were published in 1835.

FOUR TALES

James Hogg

3

CANONGATE POCKET CLASSICS

First published as a Pocket Classic in 2001 by Canongate Books Ltd, 14 High Street, Edinburgh EH1 1TE.

'The Brownie of the Black Haggs' and 'Mary Burnet' from *The Shepherd's Calendar* by James Hogg, The Stirling/South Carolina Edition of The Collected Works of James Hogg, edited by Douglas S. Mack, © Edinburgh University Press, 1995.

The publishers gratefully acknowledge general subsidy from the Scottish Arts Council towards the Canongate Classics and Pocket Classics Series.

Typeset in 10pt Plantin by Palimpsest Book Production Limited, Polmont, Stirlingshire.

Printed and bound by Omnia Books, Glasgow.

10 9 8 7 6 5 4 3 2 1

CANONGATE CLASSICS
Series Editor: Roderick Watson
Editorial Board: John Pick, Cairns Craig,
Dorothy McMillan

British Library Cataloguing-in-Publication Data
A catalogue record for this volume is available on request from the British Library.

ISBN 1 84195 158 7

www.canongate.net

The Brownie of the Black Haggs

WHEN THE SPROTS were lairds of Wheelhope, which is now a long time ago, there was one of the ladies who was very badly spoken of in the country. People did not just openly assert that Lady Wheelhope was a witch, but every one had an aversion even at hearing her named; and when by chance she happened to be mentioned, old men would shake their heads and say, 'Ah! let us alane o' her! The less ye meddle wi' her the better.' Auld wives would give over spinning, and, as a pretence for hearing what might be said about her, poke in the fire with the tongs, cocking up their ears all the while; and then, after some meaning coughs, hems, and haws, would haply say, 'Hech-wow, sirs! An a' be true that's said!' or something equally wise and decisive as that.

In short, Lady Wheelhope was accounted a very bad woman. She was an inexorable tyrant in her family, quarrelled with her servants, often cursing them, striking them, and turning them away; especially if they were religious, for these she could not endure, but suspected them of every thing bad. Whenever she found out any of the servant men of the laird's establishment for religious characters, she soon gave them up to the military, and got them shot; and several girls that were regular in their devotions, she was supposed to have popped off with poison. She was certainly a wicked woman, else many good people were mistaken in her character, and the poor persecuted Covenanters were obliged to unite in their prayers against her.

As for the laird, he was a stump. A big, dun-faced, pluffy body, that cared neither for good nor evil, and did not well know the one from the other. He laughed at his lady's tantrums and barley-hoods; and the greater the rage that she got into, the laird thought it the better sport. One day, when two servant maids came running to him, in great agitation, and told him that his lady had felled one of their companions, the laird laughed heartily at them, and said he did not doubt it.

'Why, sir, how can you laugh?' said they. 'The poor girl is killed.'

'Very likely, very likely,' said the laird. 'Well, it will teach her to take care who she angers again.'

'And, sir, your lady will be hanged.'

'Very likely; well, it will learn her how to strike so rashly again – Ha, ha, ha! Will it not, Jessy?'

But when this same Jessy died suddenly one morning, the laird was greatly confounded, and seemed dimly to comprehend that there had been unfair play going. There was little doubt that she was taken off by poison; but whether the lady did it through jealousy or not, was never divulged; but it greatly bamboozled and astonished the poor laird, for his nerves failed him, and his whole frame became paralytic. He seems to have been exactly in the same state of mind with a colley that I once had. He was extremely fond of the gun as long as I did not kill any thing with her, (there being no game laws in Ettrick Forest in those days,) and he got a grand chase after the hares when I missed them. But there was one day that I chanced for a marvel to shoot one dead, a few paces before his nose. I'll never forget the astonishment that the poor beast manifested. He stared one while at the gun, and another while at the dead hare, and seemed to be drawing the conclusion, that if the case stood thus, there was no creature sure of its life. Finally, he took his tail between his legs, and ran away home, and never would face a gun all his life again.

So was it precisely with Laird Sprot of Wheelhope. As long as his lady's wrath produced only noise and splutter among the servants, he thought it fine sport; but when he saw what he believed the dreadful effects of it, he became like a barrel organ out of tune, and could only discourse one note, which he did to every one he met. 'I wish she maunna hae gotten something she has been the waur of.' This note he repeated early and late, night and day, sleeping and waking, alone and in company, from the moment that Jessy died till she was buried; and on going to the churchyard as chief mourner, he whispered it to her relations by the way. When they came to the grave, he took his stand at the head, nor would he give place to the girl's father; but there he stood, like a huge post, as though he neither saw nor heard; and when he had lowered her late comely head into the grave, and dropped the cord, he slowly lifted his hat with one hand, wiped his dim eyes with the back of the other, and said, in a deep tremulous tone, 'Poor lassie! I wish she didna get something she had been the waur of.'

This death made a great noise among the common people; but there was no protection for the life of the subject in those days; and provided a man or woman was a true loyal subject, and a real Anti-Covenanter, any of them might kill as many as they liked. So there was no one to take cognizance of the circumstances relating to the death of poor Jessy.

After this, the lady walked softly for the space of two or three years. She saw that she had rendered herself odious, and had entirely lost her husband's countenance, which she liked worst of all. But the evil propensity could not be overcome; and a poor boy, whom the laird, out of sheer compassion, had taken into his service, being found dead one morning, the country people could no longer be restrained; so they went in a body to the Sheriff, and insisted on an investigation. It was proved that she detested the boy, had often threatened him, and had given him brose and butter the afternoon before he died; but the cause was ultimately dismissed, and the pursuers fined.

No one can tell to what height of wickedness she might now have proceeded, had not a check of a very singular kind been laid upon her. Among the servants that came home at the next term, was one who called himself Merodach; and a strange person he was. He had the form of a boy, but the features of one a hundred years old, save that his eyes had a brilliancy and restlessness, which was very extraordinary, bearing a strong resemblance to the eyes of a well-known species of monkey. He was froward and perverse in all his actions, and disregarded the pleasure or displeasure of any person; but he performed his work well, and with apparent ease. From the moment that he entered the house, the lady conceived a mortal antipathy against him, and besought the laird to turn him away. But the laird, of himself, never turned away any body, and moreover he had hired him for a trivial wage, and the fellow neither wanted activity nor perseverance. The natural consequence of this arrangement was, that the lady instantly set herself to make Merodach's life as bitter as it was possible, in order to get early quit of a domestic every way so disgusting. Her hatred of him was not like a common antipathy entertained by one human being against another, – she hated him as one might hate a toad or an adder; and his occupation of jotteryman (as the laird termed his servant of all work) keeping him always about her hand, it must have proved highly disagreeable.

She scolded him, she raged at him, but he only mocked her wrath, and giggled and laughed at her, with the most provoking derision. She tried to fell him again and again, but never, with all her address, could she hit him; and never did she make a blow at him, that she did not repent it. She was heavy and unwieldy, and he as quick in his motions as a monkey; besides, he generally had her in such an ungovernable rage, that when she flew at him, she hardly knew what she was doing. At one time she guided her blow towards him, and he at the same instant avoided it with such dexterity, that she knocked down the chief hind, or foresman; and then Merodach giggled so heartily, that, lifting the kitchen poker, she threw it at him with a full design of knocking out his brains; but the missile only broke every plate and ashet on the kitchen dresser.

She then hasted to the laird, crying bitterly, and telling him she would not suffer that wretch Merodach, as she called him, to stay another night in the family. 'Why, then, put him away, and trouble me no more about him,' said the laird.

'Put him away!' exclaimed she; 'I have already ordered him away a hundred times, and charged him never to let me see his horrible face again; but he only flouts me, and tells me he'll see me at the devil first.'

The pertinacity of the fellow amused the laird exceedingly; his dim eyes turned upwards into his head with delight; he then looked two ways at once, turned round his back, and laughed till the tears ran down his dun cheeks, but he could only articulate 'You're fitted now.'

The lady's agony of rage still increasing from this derision, she flew on the laird, and said he was not worthy the name of a man, if he did not turn away that pestilence, after the way he had abused her.

'Why, Shusy, my dear, what has he done to you?'

'What done to me! has he not caused me to knock down John Thomson, and I do not know if ever he will come to life again?'

'Have you felled your favourite John Thomson?'

said the laird, laughing more heartily than before; 'you might have done a worse deed than that. But what evil has John done?'

'And has he not broke every plate and dish on the whole dresser?' continued the lady, disregarding the laird's question; 'and for all this devastation, he only mocks at my displeasure, – absolutely mocks me, – and if you do not have him turned away, and hanged or shot for his deeds, you are not worthy the name of man.'

'O alack! What a devastation among the china metal!' said the laird; and calling on Merodach, he said, 'Tell me, thou evil Merodach of Babylon, how thou dared'st knock down thy lady's favourite servant, John Thomson?'

'Not I, your honour. It was my lady herself, who got into such a furious rage at me, that she mistook her man, and felled Mr Thomson; and the good man's skull is fractured.'

'That was very odd,' said the laird, chuckling; 'I do not comprehend it. But then, what the devil set you on smashing all my lady's delft and china ware? – That was a most infamous and provoking action.'

'It was she herself, your honour. Sorry would I have been to have broken one dish belonging to the house. I take all the house-servants to witness, that my lady smashed all the dishes with a poker, and now lays the blame on me.'

The laird turned his dim and delighted eyes on his lady, who was crying with vexation and rage, and seemed meditating another personal attack on the culprit, which he did not at all appear to shun, but rather encourage. She, however, vented her wrath in threatenings of the most deep and desperate revenge, the creature all the while assuring her that she would be foiled, and that in all her encounters and contests with him, she would uniformly come to the worst. He was resolved to do his duty, and there before his master he defied her.

The laird thought more than he considered it prudent to reveal; but he had little doubt that his wife would wreak that vengeance on his jotteryman which she avowed, and as little of her capability. He almost shuddered when he recollected one who had taken *something that she had been the waur of.*

In a word, the Lady of Wheelhope's inveterate malignity against this one object, was like the rod of Moses, that swallowed up the rest of the serpents. All her wicked and evil propensities seemed to be superseded by it, if not utterly absorbed in its virtues. The rest of the family now lived in comparative peace and quietness; for early and late her malevolence was venting itself against the jotteryman, and him alone.

It was a delirium of hatred and vengeance, on which the whole bent and bias of her inclination was set. She could not stay from the creature's presence, for in the intervals when absent from him, she spent her breath in curses and execrations, and then not able to rest, she ran again to seek him, her eyes gleaming with the anticipated delights of vengeance, while, ever and anon, all the scaith, the ridicule, and the harm, redounded on herself.

Was it not strange that she could not get quit of this sole annoyance of her life? One would have thought she easily might. But by this time there was nothing farther from her intention; she wanted vengeance, full, adequate, and delicious vengeance, on her audacious opponent. But he was a strange and terrible creature, and the means of retaliation came always, as it were, to his hand.

Bread and sweet milk was the only fare that Merodach cared for, and he having bargained for that, would not want it, though he often got it with a curse and with ill will. The lady having intentionally kept back his wonted allowance for some days, on the Sabbath morning following, she set him down a bowl of rich sweet milk, well drugged with a deadly poison, and then she lingered in a little anteroom to watch the success of her grand plot, and prevent any other creature from tasting of the potion. Merodach came in, and the house-maid says to him, 'There is your breakfast, creature.'

'Oho! my lady has been liberal this morning,' said he; 'but I am beforehand with her. – Here, little Missie, you seem very hungry today – take you my breakfast.' And with that he set the beverage down to the lady's little favourite spaniel. It so happened that the lady's only son came at that instant into the anteroom, seeking her, and teazing his mamma about something which took her attention from the hall-table for a space. When she looked again, and saw Missie lapping up the sweet milk, she burst from her lobby like a dragon, screaming as if her head had been on fire, kicked the bowl and the remainder of its contents against the wall, and lifting Missie in her bosom, she retreated hastily, crying all the way.

'Ha, ha, ha – I have you now!' cried Merodach, as she vanished from the hall.

Poor Missie died immediately, and very privately; indeed, she would have died and been buried, and never one have seen her, save her mistress, had not Merodach, by a luck that never failed him, popped his nose over the flower garden wall, just as his lady was laying her favourite in a grave of her own digging. She, not perceiving her tormentor, plied on at her task, apostrophising the insensate little carcass, –

'Ah! poor dear little creature, thou hast had a hard
fortune, and hast drank of the bitter potion that was
not intended for thee; but he shall drink it three times
double, for thy sake!'

'Is that little Missie?' said the eldrich voice of the
jotteryman, close at the lady's ear. She uttered a loud
scream, and sunk down on the bank. 'Alack for poor
little Missie!' continued the creature in a tone of
mockery, 'My heart is sorry for Missie. What has
befallen her – whose breakfast cup did she drink?'

'Hence with thee, thou fiend!' cried the lady; 'what
right hast thou to intrude on thy mistress's privacy?
Thy turn is coming yet, or may the nature of woman
change within me.'

'It is changed already,' said the creature, grinning
with delight; 'I have thee now, I have thee now! And
were it not to shew my superiority over thee, which
I do every hour, I should soon see thee strapped like
a mad cat, or a worrying bratch. What wilt thou
try next?'

'I will cut thy throat, and if I die for it, will rejoice
in the deed; a deed of charity to all that dwell on the
face of the earth. Go about thy business.'

'I have warned thee before, dame, and I now warn
thee again, that all thy mischief meditated against me
will fall double on thine own head.'

'I want none of your warning, and none of your

instructions, fiendish cur. Hence with your elvish face, and take care of yourself.'

It would be too disgusting and horrible to relate or read all the incidents that fell out between this unaccountable couple. Their enmity against each other had no end, and no mitigation; and scarcely a single day passed over on which her acts of malevolent ingenuity did not terminate fatally for some favourite thing of the lady's, while all these doings never failed to appear as her own act. Scarcely was there a thing, animate or inanimate, on which she set a value, left to her, that was not destroyed; and yet scarcely one hour or minute could she remain absent from her tormentor, and all the while, it seems, solely for the purpose of tormenting him.

But while all the rest of the establishment enjoyed peace and quietness from the fury of their termagant dame, matters still grew worse and worse between the fascinated pair. The lady haunted the menial, in the same manner as the raven haunts the eagle, for a perpetual quarrel, though the former knows that in every encounter she is to come off the loser. But now noises were heard on the stairs by night, and it was whispered among the menials, that the lady had been seeking Merodach's bed by night, on some horrible intent. Several of them would have sworn that they had seen her passing and repassing on the stair after midnight, when all was quiet; but then it was likewise well known, that Merodach slept with well fastened doors, and a companion in another bed in the same room, whose bed, too, was nearest the door. Nobody cared much what became of the jotteryman, for he was an unsocial and disagreeable person; but some one told him what they had seen, and hinted a suspicion of the lady's intent. But the creature only bit his upper lip, winked with his eyes, and said, 'She had better let alone; she will be the first to rue that.'

Not long after this, to the horror of the family and the whole country side, the laird's only son was found murdered in his bed one morning, under circumstances that manifested the most fiendish cruelty and inveteracy on the part of his destroyer. As soon as the atrocious act was divulged, the lady fell into convulsions, and lost her reason; and happy had it been for her had she never recovered either the use of reason, or her corporeal functions any more, for there was blood upon her hand, which she took no care to conceal, and there was too little doubt that it was the blood of her own innocent and beloved boy, the sole heir and hope of the family.

This blow deprived the laird of all power of action; but the lady had a brother, a man of the law, who came and instantly proceeded to an investigation of this unaccountable murder; but before the Sheriff arrived, the housekeeper took the lady's brother aside, and told him he had better not go on with the scrutiny, for she was sure the crime would be brought home to her unfortunate mistress; and after examining into several corroborative circumstances, and viewing the state of the raving maniac, with the blood on her hand and arm, he made the investigation a very short one, declaring the domestics all exculpated.

The laird attended his boy's funeral, and laid his head in the grave, but appeared exactly like a man walking in a trance, an automaton, without feelings or sensations, oftentimes gazing at the funeral procession, as on something he could not comprehend. And when the death-bell of the parish church fell a-tolling, as the corpse approached the kirk-stile, he cast a dim eye up towards the belfry, and said hastily, 'What, what's that? Och ay, we're just in time, just in time.' And often was he hammering over the name of 'Evil Merodach, King of Babylon,' to himself. He seemed to have some far-fetched conception that his unaccountable jotteryman had a hand in the death of his only son, and other lesser calamities, although the evidence in favour of Merodach's innocence was as usual quite decisive.

This grievous mistake of Lady Wheelhope (for every landward laird's wife was then styled Lady) can only be accounted for, by supposing her in a state of derangement, or rather under some evil influence, over which she had no control; and to a person in such a state, the mistake was not so very unnatural. The mansion-house of Wheelhope was old and irregular. The stair had four acute turns, all the same, and four landing-places, all the same. In the uppermost chamber slept the two domestics, – Merodach in the bed farthest in, and in the chamber immediately below that, which was exactly similar, slept the young laird and his tutor, the former in the bed farthest in; and thus, in the turmoil of raging passions, her own hand made herself childless.

Merodach was expelled the family forthwith, but refused to accept of his wages, which the man of law pressed upon him, for fear of farther mischief; but he went away in apparent sullenness and discontent, no one knowing whither.

When his dismissal was announced to the lady, who was watched day and night in her chamber, the news had such an effect on her, that her whole frame seemed electrified; the horrors of remorse vanished, and another passion, which I neither can comprehend nor define, took the sole possession of her distempered spirit. 'He *must* not go! – He *shall* not go!' she exclaimed. 'No, no, no – he shall not – he shall not – he shall not!' and then she instantly set herself about making ready to follow him, uttering all

the while the most diabolical expressions, indicative
of anticipated vengeance. – 'Oh, could I but snap his
nerves one by one, and birl among his vitals! Could I
but slice his heart off piecemeal in small messes, and see
his blood lopper and bubble, and spin away in purple
slays; and then to see him grin, and grin, and grin, and
grin! Oh – oh – oh – How beautiful and grand a sight it
would be to see him grin, and grin, and grin!' And in
such a style would she run on for hours together.

She thought of nothing, she spake of nothing, but
the discarded jotteryman, whom most people now
began to regard as a creature that was not canny.
They had seen him eat, and drink, and work like
other people; still he had that about him that was
not like other men. He was a boy in form, and
an antediluvian in feature. Some thought he was
a mule, between a Jew and an ape; some a wiz-
ard, some a kelpie, or a fairy, but most of all, that
he was really and truly a Brownie. What he was
I do not know, and therefore will not pretend to
say; but be that as it may, in spite of locks and
keys, watching and waking, the Lady of Wheelhope
soon made her escape and eloped after him. The
attendants, indeed, would have made oath that she
was carried away by some invisible hand, for that it
was impossible she could have escaped on foot like
other people; and this edition of the story took in

the country; but sensible people viewed the matter
in another light.

As for instance, when Wattie Blythe, the laird's old
shepherd, came in from the hill one morning, his wife
Bessie thus accosted him. – 'His presence be about us,
Wattie Blythe! have ye heard what has happened at the
ha'? Things are aye turning waur and waur there, and it
looks like as if Providence had gi'en up our laird's
house to destruction. This grand estate maun now
gang frae the Sprots, for it has finished them.'

'Na, na, Bessie, it isna the estate that has finished the
Sprots, but the Sprots that hae finished it, an' themsells
into the boot. They hae been a wicked and degenerate
race, an' aye the langer the waur, till they hae reached
the utmost bounds o' earthly wickedness; an' it's time
the deil were looking after his ain.'

'Ah, Wattie Blythe, ye never said a truer say. An'
that's just the very point where your story ends, and
mine commences; for hasna the deil, or the fairies, or
the brownies, ta'en away our lady bodily, an' the haill
country is running and riding in search o' her; and there
is twenty hunder merks offered to the first that can find
her, an' bring her safe back. They hae ta'en her away,
skin an' bane, body an' soul, an' a', Wattie!'

'Hech-wow! but that is awsome! And where is it
thought they have ta'en her to, Bessie?'

'O, they hae some guess at that frae her ain hints

afore. It is thought they hae carried her after that Satan of a creature, wha wrought sae muckle wae about the house. It is for him they are a' looking, for they ken weel, that where they get the tane they will get the tither.'

'Whew! Is that the gate o't, Bessie? Why, then, the awfu' story is nouther mair nor less than this, that the leddy has made a lopment, as they ca't, and run away after a blackgaird jotteryman. Hech-wow! wae's me for human frailty! But that's just the gate! When aince the deil gets in the point o' his finger, he will soon have in his haill hand. Ay, he wants but a hair to make a tether of, ony day. I hae seen her a braw sonsy lass, but even then I feared she was devoted to destruction, for she aye mockit at religion, Bessie, an' that's no a good mark of a young body. An' she made a' its servants her enemies; an' think you these good men's prayers were a' to blaw away i' the wind, and be nae mair regarded? Na, na, Bessie, my woman, take ye this mark baith o' our ain bairns and ither folk's – If ever ye see a young body that disregards the Sabbath, and makes a mock at the ordinances o' religion, ye will never see that body come to muckle good. A braw hand she has made o' her gibes an' jeers at religion, an' her mockeries o' the poor persecuted hill-folk! – sunk down by degrees into the very dregs o' sin and misery! run away after a scullion!'

'Fy, fy, Wattie, how can ye say sae? It was weel kenn'd that she hatit him wi' a perfect an' mortal hatred, an' tried to make away wi' him mae ways nor ane.'

'Aha, Bessie; but nipping an' scarting are Scots folk's wooing; an' though it is but right that we suspend our judgments, there will naebody persuade me, if she be found alang wi' the creature, but that she has run away after him in the natural way, on her twa shanks, without help either frae fairy or brownie.'

'I'll never believe sic a thing of any woman born, let be a lady weel up in years.'

'Od help ye, Bessie! ye dinna ken the stretch o' corrupt nature. The best o' us, when left to oursells, are nae better than strayed sheep, that will never find the way back to their ain pastures; an' of a' things made o' mortal flesh, a wicked woman is the warst.'

'Alack-a-day! we get the blame o' muckle that we little deserve. But, Wattie, keep ye a gayan sharp look-out about the cleuchs and the caves o' our glen, or hope, as ye ca't; for the lady kens them a' gayan weel; and gin the twenty hunder merks wad come our way, it might gang a waur gate. It wad tocher a' our bonny lasses.'

'Ay, weel I wat, Bessie, that's nae lee. And now, when ye bring me amind o't, the L—— forgie me gin I didna hear a creature up in the Brock-holes this morning, skirling as if something war cutting its throat. It gars a' the hairs stand on my head when I think it may hae been our leddy, an' the droich of a creature murdering her. I took it for a battle of wulcats, and wished they might pu' out ane anither's thrapples; but when I think on it again, they war unco like some o' our leddy's unearthly screams.'

'His presence be about us, Wattie! Haste ye. Pit on your bonnet – take your staff in your hand, and gang an' see what it is.'

'Shame fa' me, if I daur gang, Bessie.'

'Hout, Wattie, trust in the Lord.'

'Aweel, sae I do. But ane's no to throw himself ower a linn, an' trust that the Lord's to kep him in a blanket; nor hing himsell up in a raip, an' expect the Lord to come and cut him down. An' it's nae muckle safer for an auld stiff man to gang away out to a wild remote place, where there is ae body murdering another. – What is that I hear, Bessie? Haud the lang tongue o' you, and rin to the door, an' see what noise that is.'

Bessie ran to the door, but soon returned an altered creature, with her mouth wide open, and her eyes set in her head.

'It is them, Wattie! it is them! His presence be about us! What will we do?'

'Them? whaten them?'

'Why, that blackguard creature, coming here, leading our leddy be the hair o' the head, an' yerking her wi' a stick. I am terrified out o' my wits. What will we do?'

'We'll *see* what they *say*,' said Wattie, manifestly in as great terror as his wife; and by a natural impulse, or as a last resource, he opened the Bible, not knowing what he did, and then hurried on his spectacles; but before he got two leaves turned over, the two entered, a frightful-looking couple indeed. Merodach, with his old withered face, and ferret eyes, leading the Lady of Wheelhope by the long hair, which was mixed with grey, and whose face was all bloated with wounds and bruises, and having stripes of blood on her garments.

'How's this! – How's this, sirs?' said Wattie Blythe.

'Close that book, and I will tell you, goodman,' said Merodach.

'I can hear what you hae to say wi' the beuk open, sir,' said Wattie, turning over the leaves, as if looking for some particular passage, but apparently not knowing what he was doing. 'It is a shamefu' business this, but some will hae to answer for't. My leddy, I am unco grieved to see you in sic a plight. Ye hae surely been dooms sair left to yourself.'

The lady shook her head, uttered a feeble hollow laugh, and fixed her eyes on Merodach. But such a look! It almost frightened the simple aged couple out of their senses. It was not a look of love nor of hatred exclusively; neither was it of desire or disgust, but it was a combination of them all. It was such a look as one fiend would cast on another, in whose everlasting destruction he rejoiced. Wattie was glad to take his eyes from such countenances, and look into the Bible, that firm foundation of all his hopes and all his joy.

'I request that you will shut that book, sir,' said the horrible creature; 'or if you do not, I will shut it for you with a vengeance;' and with that he seized it, and flung it against the wall. Bessie uttered a scream, and Wattie was quite paralysed; and although he seemed disposed to run after his best friend, as he called it, the hellish looks of the Brownie interposed, and glued him to his seat.

'Hear what I have to say first,' said the creature, 'and then pore your fill on that precious book of yours. One concern at a time is enough. I came to do you a service. Here, take this cursed, wretched woman, whom you style your lady, and deliver her up to the lawful authorities, to be restored to her husband and her place in society. She is come upon one that hates her, and never said one kind word to her in his life, and though I have beat her like a dog, still she clings to me, and will not depart, so enchanted is she with the laudable purpose of cutting my throat. Tell your master and her brother, that I am not to be burdened with their maniac. I have scourged, I have spurned and kicked her, afflicting her night and day, and yet from my side she will not depart. Take her. Claim the reward in full, and your fortune is made, and so farewell.'

The creature bowed and went away, but the moment his back was turned the lady fell a-screaming and struggling like one in an agony, and, in spite of all the old couple's exertions, she forced herself out of their hands, and ran after the retreating Merodach. When he saw better would not be, he turned upon her, and, by one blow with his stick, struck her down; and, not content with that, he continued to kick and baste her in such a manner as to all appearance would have killed twenty ordinary persons. The poor devoted dame could do nothing, but now and then utter a squeak like a half-worried cat, and writhe and grovel on the sward, till Wattie and his wife came up and withheld her tormentor from further violence. He then bound her hands behind her back with a strong cord, and delivered her once more to the charge of the old couple, who contrived to hold her by that means and take her home.

Wattie had not the face to take her into the hall, but into one of the outhouses, where he brought her brother to receive her. The man of the law was manifestly vexed at her reappearance, and scrupled not to testify his dissatisfaction; for when Wattie told him how the wretch had abused his sister, and that, had it not been for Bessie's interference and his own, the lady would have been killed outright,

'Why, Walter, it is a great pity that he did not kill her outright,' said he. 'What good can her life now do to her, or of what value is her life to any creature living? After one has lived to disgrace all connected with them, the sooner they are taken off the better.'

The man, however, paid old Walter down his two thousand merks, a great fortune for one like him in those days; and not to dwell longer on this unnatural story, I shall only add, very shortly, that the Lady of Wheelhope soon made her escape once more, and flew, as by an irresistible charm, to her tormentor. Her friends looked no more after her; and the last time she was seen alive, it was following the uncouth creature up the water of Daur, weary, wounded, and lame, while he was all the way beating her, as a piece of excellent amusement. A few days after that, her body was found among some wild haggs, in a place called Crook-burn, by a party of the persecuted Covenanters that were in hiding there, some of the very men whom she had exerted herself to destroy, and who had been driven, like David of old, to pray for a curse and earthly punishment upon her. They buried her like a dog at the Yetts of Keppel, and rolled three huge stones upon her grave, which are lying there to this day. When they found her corpse, it was mangled and wounded in a most shocking manner, the fiendish creature having manifestly tormented her to death. He was never more seen or heard of in this kingdom, though all that country-side was kept in terror for him many years afterwards; and to this day, they will tell you of THE BROWNIE OF THE BLACK HAGGS, which title he seems to have acquired after his disappearance.

This story was told to me by an old man, named Adam Halliday, whose great grandfather, Thomas Halliday, was one of those that found the body and buried it. It is many years since I heard it; but, however ridiculous it may appear, I remember it made a dreadful impression on my young mind. I never heard any story like it, save one of an old fox-hound that pursued a fox through the Grampians for a fortnight, and when at last discovered by the Duke of Athole's people, neither of them could run, but the hound was still continuing to walk after the fox, and when the latter lay down the other lay down beside him, and looked at him steadily all the while, though unable to do him the least harm. The passion of inveterate malice seems to have influenced these two exactly alike. But, upon the whole, I scarcely believe the tale can be true.

The Cameronian Preacher's Tale

SIT NEAR ME, my children, and come nigh, all ye who are not of my kindred, though of my flock; for my days and hours are numbered; death is with me dealing, and I have a sad and a wonderful story to relate. I have preached and ye have profited; but what I am about to say is far better than man's preaching, it is one of those terrible sermons which God preaches to mankind, of blood unrighteously shed, and most wondrously avenged. The like has not happened in these our latter days. His presence is visible in it; and I reveal it that its burthen may be removed from my soul, so that I may die in peace; and I disclose it, that you may lay it up in your hearts and tell it soberly to your children, that the warning memory of a dispensation so marvellous may live and not perish. Of the deed itself, some of you have heard a whispering; and some of you know the men of whom I am about to speak; but the mystery which covers them up as with a cloud I shall remove; listen, therefore, my children, to a tale of truth, and may you profit by it!

On Dryfe Water, in Annandale, lived Walter Johnstone, a man open hearted and kindly, but proud withal and warm tempered; and on the same water lived John Macmillan, a man of a nature grasping and sordid, and as proud and hot tempered as the other. They were strong men, and vain of their strength; lovers of pleasant company, well to live in the world, extensive dealers in corn and cattle; married too, and both of the same age – five and forty years. They often met, yet they were not friends; nor yet were they companions, for bargain making and money seeking narroweth the heart and shuts up generosity of soul. They were jealous, too, of one another's success in trade, and of the fame they had each acquired for feats of personal strength and agility, and skill with the sword – a weapon which all men carried, in my youth, who were above the condition of a peasant. Their mutual and growing dislike was inflamed by the whisperings of evil friends, and confirmed by the skilful manner in which they negotiated bargains over each other's heads. When they met, a short and surly greeting was exchanged, and those who knew their natures looked for a meeting between them, when the sword or some other dangerous weapon would settle for ever their claims for precedence in cunning and in strength.

They met at the fair of Longtown, and spoke, and no more – with them both it was a busy day, and mutual hatred subsided for a time, in the love of turning the penny and amassing gain. The market rose and fell, and fell and rose; and it was whispered that Macmillan, through the superior skill or good fortune of his rival, had missed some bargains which were very valuable, while some positive losses touched a nature extremely sensible of the importance of wealth. One was elated and the other depressed – but not more depressed than moody and incensed, and in this temper they were seen in the evening in the back room of a public inn, seated apart and silent, calculating losses and gains, drinking deeply, and exchanging dark looks of hatred and distrust. They had been observed, during the whole day, to watch each other's movements, and now when they were met face to face, the labours of the day over, and their natures inflamed by liquor as well as by hatred, their companions looked for personal strife between them, and wondered not a little when they saw Johnstone rise, mount his horse, and ride homewards, leaving his rival in Longtown. Soon afterwards Macmillan started up from a moody fit, drank off a large draught of brandy, threw down a half-guinea, nor waited for change – a thing uncommon with him; and men said, as his horse's feet struck fire from the pavement, that if he overtook Johnstone, there would be a living soul less in the land before sunrise.

Before sunrise next morning the horse of Walter Johnstone came with an empty saddle to his stable door. The bridle was trampled to pieces amongst its feet, and its saddle and sides were splashed over with blood as if a bleeding body had been carried across its back. The cry arose in the country, an instant search was made, and on the side of the public road was found a place where a deadly contest seemed to have happened. It was in a small green field, bordered by a wood, in the farm of Andrew Pattison. The sod was dinted deep with men's feet, and trodden down and trampled and sprinkled over with blood as thickly as it had ever been with dew. Blood drops, too, were traced to some distance, but nothing more was discovered; the body could not be found, though every field was examined and every pool dragged. His money and bills, to the amount of several thousand pounds, were gone, so was his sword – indeed nothing of him could be found on earth save his blood, and for its spilling a strict account was yet to be sought.

Suspicion instantly and naturally fell on John Macmillan, who denied all knowledge of the deed. He had arrived at his own house in due course of time, no marks of weapon or warfare were on him, he performed family worship as was his custom, and he sang the psalm as loudly and prayed as fervently as he was in the habit of doing. He was apprehended and tried, and saved by the contradictory testimony of the witnesses against him, into whose hearts the spirit of falsehood seemed to have entered in order to perplex and confound the judgment of men – or rather that man might have no hand in the punishment, but that God should bring it about in his own good time and way. 'Revenge is mine, saith the Lord,' which meaneth not because it is too sweet a morsel for man, as the scoffer said, but because it is too dangerous. A glance over this conflicting testimony will show how little was then known of this foul offence, and how that little was rendered doubtful and dark by the imperfections of human nature.

Two men of Longtown were examined. One said that he saw Macmillan insulting and menacing Johnstone, laying his hand on the hilt of his sword with a look dark and ominous; while the other swore that he was present at the time, but that it was Johnstone who insulted and menaced Macmillan, and laid his hand on the hilt of his sword and pointed to the road homewards. A very expert and searching examination could make no more of them; they were both respectable men with characters above suspicion. The next witnesses were of another stamp, and their testimony was circuitous and contradictory. One of them was a shepherd – a reluctant witness. His words were these: 'I was frae hame on the night of the murder, in the thick of the wood, no just at the place which was bloody and trampled, but gaye and near hand it. I canna say I can just mind what I was doing; I had somebody to see I jalouse, but wha it was is naebody's business but my ain. There was maybe ane forbye myself in the wood, and maybe twa; there was ane at ony rate, and I am no sure but it was an auld acquaintance. I see nae use there can be in questioning me. I saw nought, and therefore can say nought. I canna but say that I heard something – the trampling of horses, and a rough voice saying, "Draw and defend yourself." Then followed the clashing of swords and half smothered sort of work, and then the sound of horses' feet was heard again, and that's a' I ken about it; only I thought the voice was Walter Johnstone's, and so thought Kate Pennie, who was with me and kens as meikle as me.' The examination of Katherine Pennie, one of the Pennies of Pennieland, followed, and she declared that she had heard the evidence of Dick Purdie with surprise and anger. On that night she was not over the step of her father's door for more than five minutes, and that was to look at the sheep in the fauld; and she neither heard the clashing of swords nor the word of man or woman. And with respect to Dick Purdie, she scarcely knew him even by sight; and if all tales were true that were told of him, she would not venture into a lonely wood with him, under the cloud of night, for a gown of silk with pearls on each sleeve. The shepherd, when recalled, admitted that Kate Pennie might be right, 'For after a',' said he, 'it happened in the dark, when a man like me, no that gleg of the uptauk, might confound persons. Somebody was with me, I am gaye and sure, frae what took place – if it was nae Kate, I kenna wha it was, and it couldna weel be Kate either, for Kate's a douce quean, and besides is married.' The judge dismissed the witnesses with some indignant words, and, turning to the prisoner, said, 'John Macmillan, the prevarications of these witnesses have saved you; mark my words – saved you from man, but not from God. On the murderer, the Most High will lay his hot right hand, visibly and before men, that we may know that blood unjustly shed will be avenged. You are at liberty to depart.' He left the bar and resumed his station and his pursuits as usual; nor did he appear sensible to the feeling of the country, which was strong against him.

A year passed over his head, other events happened, and the murder of Walter Johnstone began to be dismissed from men's minds. Macmillan went to the fair of Longtown, and when evening came he was seated in the little back room which I mentioned before, and in company with two men of the names of Hunter and Hope. He sat late, drank deeply, but in the midst of the carousal a knock was heard at the door, and a voice called sharply, 'John Macmillan.' He started up, seemed alarmed, and exclaimed, 'What in Heaven's name can *he* want with me?' and opening the door hastily, went into the garden, for he seemed to dread another summons lest his companions should know the voice. As soon as he was gone, one said to the other, 'If that was not the voice of Walter Johnstone, I never heard it in my life; he is either come back in the flesh or in the spirit, and in either way John Macmillan has good cause to dread him.' They listened – they heard Macmillan speaking in great agitation; he was answered only by a low sound, yet he appeared to understand what was said, for his concluding words were, 'Never! never! I shall rather submit to His judgment who cannot err.' When he returned he was pale and shaking, and he sat down and seemed buried in thought. He spread his palms on his knees, shook his head often, then, starting up, said, 'The judge was a fool and no prophet – to mortal man is not given the wisdom of God – so neighbours let us ride.' They mounted their horses and rode homewards into Scotland at a brisk pace.

The night was pleasant, neither light nor dark; there were few travellers out, and the way winded with the hills and with the streams, passing through a pastoral and beautiful country. Macmillan rode close by the side of his companions, closer than was desirable or common; yet he did not speak, nor make answer when he was spoken to; but looked keenly and earnestly before and behind him, as if he expected the coming of some one, and every tree and bush seemed to alarm and startle him. Day at last dawned, and with the growing light his alarm subsided, and he began to converse with his companions, and talk with a levity which surprised them more than his silence had done before. The sun was all but risen when they approached the farm of Andrew Pattison, and here and there the top of a high tree and the summit of a hill had caught light upon them. Hope looked to Hunter silently, when they came nigh the bloody spot where it was believed the murder had been committed. Macmillan sat looking resolutely before him, as if determined not to look upon it; but his horse stopt at once, trembled violently, and then sprung aside, hurling its rider headlong to the ground. All this passed in a moment; his companions sat astonished; the horse rushed forward, leaving him on the ground, from whence he never rose in life, for his neck was broken by the fall, and with a convulsive shiver or two he expired. Then did the prediction of the judge, the warning voice and summons of the preceding night, and the spot and the time, rush upon their recollection; and they firmly believed that a murderer and robber lay dead beside them. 'His horse saw something,' said Hope to Hunter; 'I never saw such flashing eyes in a horse's head;' – 'and *he* saw something too,' replied Hunter, 'for the glance that he gave to the bloody spot, when his horse started, was one of terror. I never saw such a look, and I wish never to see such another again.'

When John Macmillan perished, matters stood thus with his memory. It was not only loaded with the sin of blood and the sin of robbery, with the sin of making a faithful woman a widow and her children fatherless, but with the grievous sin also of having driven a worthy family to ruin and beggary. The sum which was lost was large, the creditors were merciless; they fell upon the remaining substance of Johnstone, sweeping it wholly away; and his widow sought shelter in a miserable cottage among the Dryfesdale hills, where she supported her children

by gathering and spinning wool. In a far different
state and condition remained the family of John
Macmillan. He died rich and unincumbered, leaving an evil name and an only child, a daughter,
wedded to one whom many knew and esteemed,
Joseph Howatson by name, a man sober and sedate;
a member, too, of our own broken remnant of
Cameronians.

Now, my dear children, the person who addresses
you was then, as he is yet, God's preacher for the
scattered kirk of Scotland, and his tent was pitched
among the green hills of Annandale. The death of
the transgressor appeared unto me the manifest
judgment of God, and when my people gathered
around me I rejoiced to see so great a multitude,
and, standing in the midst of them, I preached in
such a wise that they were deeply moved. I took for
my text these words, 'Hath there been evil in the
land and the Lord hath not known it?' I discoursed
on the wisdom of Providence in guiding the affairs
of men. How he permitted our evil passions to
acquire the mastery over us, and urge us to deeds
of darkness; allowing us to flourish for a season, that
he might strike us in the midst of our splendour in
a way so visible and awful that the wildest would
cry out, 'Behold the finger of God.' I argued the
matter home to the heart; I named no names, but

I saw Joseph Howatson hide his face in his hands, for he felt and saw from the eyes which were turned towards him that I alluded to the judgment of God upon his relative.

Joseph Howatson went home heavy and sad of heart, and somewhat touched with anger at God's servant for having so pointedly and publicly alluded to his family misfortune; for he believed his father-in-law was a wise and a worthy man. His way home lay along the banks of a winding and beautiful stream, and just where it entered his own lands there was a rustic gate, over which he leaned for a little space, ruminating upon earlier days, on his wedded wife, on his children, and finally his thoughts settled on his father-in-law. He thought of his kindness to himself and to many others, on his fulfilment of all domestic duties, on his constant performance of family worship, and on his general reputation for honesty and fair dealing. He then dwelt on the circumstances of Johnstone's disappearance, on the singular summons his father-in-law received in Longtown, and the catastrophe which followed on the spot and on the very day of the year that the murder was supposed to be committed. He was in sore perplexity, and said aloud, 'Would to God that I knew the truth; but the doors of eternity, alas! are shut on the secret for ever.' He looked up and John Macmillan stood before him – stood with all the calmness and serenity and meditative air which a grave man wears when he walks out on a sabbath eve.

'Joseph Howatson,' said the apparition, 'on no secret are the doors of eternity shut – of whom were you speaking?' 'I was speaking,' answered he, 'of one who is cold and dead, and to whom you bear a strong resemblance.' 'I am he,' said the shape; 'I am John Macmillan.' 'God of heaven!' replied Joseph Howatson, 'how can that be; did I not lay his head in the grave; see it closed over him; how, therefore, can it be? Heaven permits no such visitations.' 'I entreat you, my son,' said the shape, 'to believe what I say; the end of man is not when his body goes to dust; he exists in another state, and from that state am I permitted to come to you; waste not time, which is brief, with vain doubts, I am John Macmillan.' 'Father, father,' said the young man, deeply agitated, 'answer me, did you kill and rob Walter Johnstone?' 'I did,' said the Spirit, 'and for that have I returned to earth; listen to me.' The young man was so much overpowered by a revelation thus fearfully made, that he fell insensible on the ground; and when he recovered, the moon was shining, the dews of night were upon him, and he was alone.

Joseph Howatson imagined that he had dreamed a fearful dream; and conceiving that Divine Providence had presented the truth to his fancy, he began to consider how he could secretly make reparation to the wife and children of Johnstone for the double crime of his relative. But on more mature reflection he was impressed with the belief that a spirit had appeared to him, the spirit of his father-in-law, and that his own alarm had hindered him from learning fully the secret of his visit to earth; he therefore resolved to go to the same place next sabbath night, seek rather than avoid an interview, acquaint himself with the state of bliss or woe in which the spirit was placed, and learn if by acts of affection and restitution he could soften his sufferings or augment his happiness. He went accordingly to the little rustic gate by the side of the lonely stream; he walked up and down; hour passed after hour, but he heard nothing and saw nothing save the murmuring of the brook and the hares running among the wild clover. He had resolved to return home, when something seemed to rise from the ground, as shapeless as a cloud at first, but moving with life. It assumed a form, and the appearance of John Macmillan was once more before him. The young man was nothing daunted, but looking on the spirit, said, 'I thought you just and upright and devout, and incapable of murder and robbery.' The spirit seemed to dilate as it made answer. 'The death of Walter Johnstone sits lightly upon me. We had crossed each other's purposes, we had lessened each other's gains, we had vowed revenge, we met on fair terms, tied our horses to a gate, and fought fairly and long; and when I slew him, I but did what he sought to do to me. I threw him over his horse, carried him far into the country, sought out a deep quagmire on the north side of the Snipe Knowe, in Crake's Moss, and having secured his bills and other perishable property, with the purpose of returning all to his family, I buried him in the moss, leaving his gold in his purse, and laying his cloak and his sword above him.

'Now listen, Joseph Howatson. In my private desk you will find a little key tied with red twine, take it and go to the house of Janet Mathieson in Dumfries, and underneath the hearthstone in my sleeping room you will get my strong-box, open it, it contains all the bills and bonds belonging to Walter Johnstone. Restore them to his widow. I would have restored them but for my untimely death. Inform her privily and covertly where she will find the body of her husband, so that she may bury him in the churchyard with his ancestors. Do these things, that I may have some assuagement of misery; neglect them, and you will become a world's wonder.' The spirit vanished with these words, and was seen no more.

Joseph Howatson was sorely troubled. He had communed with a spirit, he was impressed with the belief that early death awaited him; he felt a sinking of soul and a misery of body, and he sent for me to help him with counsel, and comfort him in his unexampled sorrow. I loved him and hastened to him; I found him weak and woe-begone, and the hand of God seemed to be sore upon him. He took me out to the banks of the little stream where the shape appeared to him, and having desired me to listen without interrupting him, told me how he had seen his father-in-law's spirit, and related the revelations which it had made and the commands it had laid upon him. 'And now,' he said, 'look upon me. I am young, and ten days ago I had a body strong and a mind buoyant, and gray hairs and the honours of old age seemed to await me. But ere three days pass I shall be as the clod of the valley, for he who converses with a spirit, a spirit shall he soon become. I have written down the strange tale I have told you and I put it into your hands, perform for me and for my wretched parent, the instructions which the grave yielded up its tenant to give; and may your days be long in the land, and may you grow gray-headed among your people.' I listened to his words with wonder and with awe, and I promised to obey him in all his wishes with my best and most anxious judgment. We went home together; we spent the evening in prayer. Then he set his house in order, spoke to all his children cheerfully and with a mild voice, and falling on the neck of his wife, said, 'Sarah Macmillan, you were the choice of my young heart, and you have been a wife to me kind, tender, and gentle.' He looked at his children and he looked at his wife, for his heart was too full for more words, and retired to his chamber. He was found next morning kneeling by his bedside, his hands held out as if repelling some approaching object, horror stamped on every feature, and cold and dead.

Then I felt full assurance of the truth of his communications; and as soon as the amazement which his untimely death occasioned had subsided, and his wife and little ones were somewhat comforted, I proceeded to fulfil his dying request. I found the small key tied with red twine, and I went to the house of Janet Mathieson in Dumfries, and I held up the key and said, 'Woman, knowest thou that?' and when she saw it she said, 'Full well I know it, it belonged to a jolly man and a douce, and mony a merry hour has he whiled away wi'

my servant maidens and me.' And when she saw
me lift the hearthstone, open the box, and spread
out the treasure which it contained, she held up
her hands, 'Eh! what o' gowd! what o' gowd! but
half's mine, be ye saint or sinner; John Macmillan,
douce man, aye said he had something there which
he considered as not belonging to him but to a
quiet friend; weel I wot he meant me, for I have
been a quiet friend to him and his.' I told her I
was commissioned by his daughter to remove the
property, that I was the minister of that persecuted
remnant of the true kirk called Cameronians, and
she might therefore deliver it up without fear. 'I
ken weel enough wha ye are,' said this worthless
woman, 'd'ye think I dinna ken a minister of the
kirk; I have seen meikle o' their siller in my day,
frae eighteen to fifty and aught have I caroused with
divines, Cameronians, I trow, as well as those of a
freer kirk. But touching this treasure, give me twenty
gowden pieces, else I'se gar three stamps of my foot
bring in them that will see me righted, and send you
awa to the mountains bleating like a sheep shorn in
winter.' I gave the imperious woman twenty pieces
of gold, and carried away the fatal box.

Now, when I got free of the ports of Dumfries,
I mounted my little horse and rode away into the
heart of the country, among the pastoral hills of

Dryfesdale. I carried the box on the saddle before me, and its contents awakened a train of melancholy thoughts within me. There were the papers of Walter Johnstone, corresponding to the description which the spirit gave, and marked with his initials in red ink by the hand of the man who slew him. There were two gold watches and two purses of gold, all tied with red twine, and many bills and much money to which no marks were attached. As I rode along pondering on these things, and casting about in my own mind how and by what means I should make restitution, I was aware of a morass, broad and wide, which with all its quagmires glittered in the moonlight before me. I knew I had penetrated into the centre of Dryfesdale, but I was not well acquainted with the country; I therefore drew my bridle, and looked around to see if any house was nigh, where I could find shelter for the night. I saw a small house built of turf and thatched with heather, from the window of which a faint light glimmered. I rode up, alighted, and there I found a woman in widow's weeds, with three sweet children, spinning yarn from the wool which the shepherds shear in spring from the udders of the ewes. She welcomed me, spread bread and placed milk before me. I asked a blessing, and ate and drank, and was refreshed.

Now it happened that, as I sat with the solitary

woman and her children, there came a man to
the door, and with a loud yell of dismay burst
it open and staggered forward crying, 'There's a
corse candle in Crake's Moss, and I'll be a dead
man before the morning.' 'Preserve me! piper,' said
the widow, 'ye're in a piteous taking; here is a
holy man who will speak comfort to you, and tell
you how all these are but delusions of the eye or
exhalations of nature.' 'Delusions and exhalations,
Dame Johnstone,' said the piper, 'd'ye think I dinna
ken a corse light from an elf candle, an elf candle
from a will-o'-wisp, and a will-o'-wisp from all other
lights of this wide world.' The name of the morass
and the woman's name now flashed upon me, and
I was struck with amazement and awe. I looked on
the widow, and I looked on the wandering piper,
and I said, 'Let me look on those corse lights, for
God creates nothing in vain; there is a wise purpose
in all things, and a wise aim.' And the piper said,
'Na, na; I have nae wish to see ony mair on't, a dead
light bodes the living nae gude; and I am sure if I
gang near Crake's Moss it will lair me amang the
hags and quags.' And I said, 'Foolish old man, you
are equally safe every where; the hand of the Lord
reaches round the earth, and strikes and protects
according as it was foreordained, for nothing is hid
from his eyes – come with me.' And the piper looked

strangely upon me and stirred not a foot; and I said, 'I shall go by myself;' and the woman said, 'Let me go with you, for I am sad of heart, and can look on such things without fear; for, alas! since I lost my own Walter Johnstone, pleasure is no longer pleasant: and I love to wander in lonesome places and by old churchyards.' 'Then,' said the piper, 'I darena bide my lane with the bairns; I'll go also; but O! let me strengthen my heart with ae spring on my pipes before I venture.' 'Play,' I said, 'Clavers and his Highlandmen, it is the tune to cheer ye and keep your heart up.' 'Your honour's no cannie,' said the old man; 'that's my favourite tune.' So he played it and said, 'Now I am fit to look on lights of good or evil.' And we walked into the open air.

All Crake's Moss seemed on fire; not illumined with one steady and uninterrupted light, but kindled up by fits like the northern sky with its wandering streamers. On a little bank which rose in the centre of the morass, the supernatural splendour seemed chiefly to settle; and having continued to shine for several minutes, the whole faded and left but one faint gleam behind. I fell on my knees, held up my hands to heaven, and said, 'This is of God; behold in that fearful light the finger of the Most High. Blood has been spilt, and can be no longer concealed; the point of the mariner's needle points less surely to the

north than yon living flame points to the place where
man's body has found a bloody grave. Follow me,'
and I walked down to the edge of the moss and gazed
earnestly on the spot. I knew now that I looked on
the long hidden resting place of Walter Johnstone,
and considered that the hand of God was manifest
in the way that I had been thus led blindfold into his
widow's house. I reflected for a moment on these
things; I wished to right the fatherless, yet spare
the feelings of the innocent; the supernatural light
partly showed me the way, and the words which I
now heard whispered by my companions aided in
directing the rest.

'I tell ye, Dame Johnstone,' said the piper, 'the
man's no cannie; or what's waur, he may belong to
the spiritual world himself, and do us a mischief.
Saw ye ever mortal man riding with ae spur and
carrying a silver-headed cane for a whip, wi' sic
a fleece of hair about his haffets and sic a wild
ee in his head; and then he kens a' things in the
heavens aboon and the earth beneath. He kenned
my favourite tune Clavers; I'se uphaud he's no in
the body, but ane of the souls made perfect of the
auld Covenanters whom Grahame or Grierson slew;
we're daft to follow him.' 'Fool body,' I heard the
widow say, 'I'll follow him; there's something about
that man, be he in the spirit or in the flesh, which is

pleasant and promising. O! could he but, by prayer
or other means of lawful knowledge, tell me about
my dear Walter Johnstone; thrice has he appeared
to me in dream or vision with a sorrowful look, and
weel ken I what that means.' We had now reached
the edge of the morass, and a dim and uncertain
light continued to twinkle about the green knoll
which rose in its middle. I turned suddenly round
and said, 'For a wise purpose am I come; to reveal
murder; to speak consolation to the widow and
the fatherless, and to soothe the perturbed spirits
of those whose fierce passions ended in untimely
death. Come with me; the hour is come, and I must
not do my commission negligently.' 'I kenned it,
I kenned it,' said the piper, 'he's just one of the
auld persecuted worthies risen from his red grave
to right the injured, and he'll do't discreetly; follow
him, Dame, follow him.' 'I shall follow,' said the
widow, 'I have that strength given me this night
which will bear me through all trials which mortal
flesh can endure.'

When we reached the little green hillock in the
centre of the morass, I looked to the north and soon
distinguished the place described by my friend Joseph
Howatson, where the body of Walter Johnstone was
deposited. The moon shone clear, the stars aided
us with their light, and some turfcutters having left

their spades standing near, I ordered the piper to take a spade and dig where I placed my staff. 'O dig carefully,' said the widow, 'do not be rude with mortal dust.' We dug and came to a sword; the point was broken and the blade hacked. 'It is the sword of my Walter Johnstone,' said his widow, 'I could swear to it among a thousand.' 'It is my father's sword,' said a fine dark haired boy who had followed us unperceived, 'it is my father's sword, and were he living who wrought this, he should na be lang in rueing it.' 'He is dead, my child,' I said, 'and beyond your reach, and vengeance is the Lord's.' 'O, Sir,' cried his widow, in a flood of tears, 'ye ken all things; tell me, is this my husband or no?' 'It is the body of Walter Johnstone,' I answered, 'slain by one who is passed to his account, and buried here by the hand that slew him, with his gold in his purse and his watch in his pocket.' So saying we uncovered the body, lifted it up, laid it on the grass; the embalming nature of the morass had preserved it from decay, and mother and child, with tears and with cries, named his name and lamented over him. His gold watch and his money, his cloak and his dress, were untouched and entire, and we bore him to the cottage of his widow, where with clasped hands she sat at his feet and his children at his head till the day drew nigh the dawn; I then rose and said, 'Woman, thy trials have been severe and manifold; a good wife, a good mother, and a good widow hast thou been, and thy reward will be where the blessed alone are admitted. It was revealed to me by a mysterious revelation that thy husband's body was where we found it; and I was commissioned by a voice, assuredly not of this world, to deliver thee this treasure, which is thy own, that thy children may be educated, and that bread and raiment may be thine.' And I delivered her husband's wealth into her hands, refused gold which she offered, and mounting my horse, rode over the hills and saw her no more. But I soon heard of her, for there rose a strange sound in the land, that a Good Spirit had appeared to the widow of Walter Johnstone, had disclosed where her husband's murdered body lay, had enriched her with all his lost wealth, had prayed by her side till the blessed dawn of day, and then vanished with the morning light. I closed my lips on the secret till now; and I reveal it to you, my children, that you may know there is a God who ruleth this world by wise and invisible means, and punisheth the wicked, and cheereth the humble of heart and the lowly minded.

Such was the last sermon of the good John Farley, a man whom I knew and loved. I think I see him now, with his long white hair and his look mild, eloquent, and sagacious. He was a giver of good counsel, a sayer of wise sayings, with wit at will, learning in abundance, and a gift in sarcasm which the wildest dreaded.

Mary Burnet

IN THIS CLASS of my pastoral legends, I must take a date, in some instances, a century earlier than the generality of those of the other classes, and describe a state of manners more primitive and visionary than any I have witnessed, simple and romantic as these have been; and I must likewise relate scenes so far out of the way of usual events, that the sophisticated gloss and polish thrown over the modern philosophic mind, may feel tainted by such antiquated breathings of superstition. Nevertheless, be it mine to cherish the visions that have been, as well as the hope of visions yet in reserve, far in the ocean of eternity, beyond the stars and the sun. For, after all, what is the soul of man without these? What but a cold phlegmatic influence, so inclosed within the walls of modern scepticism, as scarcely to be envied by the spirits of the beasts that perish?

However, as all my legends hitherto have been founded on facts, or are of themselves traditionary tales that seem originally to have been founded on facts, I should never have thought of putting the antiquated and visionary tales of my friends, the

Fairies and Brownies, among them, had it not been for the late advice of a highly valued friend, who held it as indispensable, that these most popular of all traditions by the shepherd's ingle-side, should have a place in his Calendar. At all events, I pledge myself to relate nothing that has not been handed down to me by tradition. How these traditions have originated, I leave to the professors of moral philosophy, in their definitions of pneumatology, to determine.

The following incidents are related as having occurred at a shepherd's house, not a hundred miles from St Mary's Loch; but, as the descendants of one of the families still reside in the vicinity, I deem it requisite to use names which cannot be recognised, save by those who have heard the story.

John Allanson, the farmer's son of Inverlawn, was a handsome, roving, and incautious young man, enthusiastic, amorous, and fond of adventure, and one who could hardly be said to fear the face of either man, woman, or spirit. Among other love adventures, he fell a-courting Mary Burnet, of Kirkstyle, a most lovely and innocent maiden, and one who had been bred up in rural simplicity. She loved him, but yet she was afraid of him; and though she had no objection to meeting with him among others as oft as convenient, yet she carefully avoided meeting him alone, though often and earnestly urged to it. One day, the sinful young man, finding an opportunity, at Our Lady's Chapel, after mass, urged his suit for a private meeting so ardently, and with so many vows of love and sacred esteem, that poor Mary was won; at least so far won, as to promise, that *perhaps* she would come and meet him.

The trysting place was a little green sequestered spot, on the very verge of the lake, well known to many an angler, and to none better than the writer of this old tale; and the set time when the King's Elwand (now foolishly termed the Belt of Orion) set his first golden knob above the hill. Allanson came too early; for his heart yearned to clasp his beloved Mary all alone; and he watched the evening autumnal sky with such eagerness and devotion, that he thought every little star that arose in the south-east the top knob of the King's Elwand; but no second one following in the regular time, he began to think the Gowden Elwand was lost for that night, or withheld by some spiteful angel, out of envy at the abundance of his promised enjoyment. The Elwand did at last arise in good earnest, and then the youth, with a heart palpitating with agitation, had nothing for it but to watch the heathery brow by which bonny Mary Burnet was to descend. No Mary

Burnet made her appearance, even although the
King's Elwand had now measured its own equivocal
length five or six times up the lift.

Young Allanson now felt all the most poignant
miseries of disappointment; and, as the story goes,
uttered in his heart some unhallowed wish, and even
repeated it so often, as to give the vagrant spirits of
the wild a malicious interest in the event. He wished
that some witch or fairy would influence his Mary to
come to him in spite of her maidenly scruples and
overstrained delicacy. In short, it is deemed that he
wished to have her there, by whatever means or
agency.

This wish was thrice repeated with all the energy
of disappointed love. It was thrice repeated, and no
more, when, behold, Mary appeared on the brae,
with wild and eccentric motions, speeding to the
appointed place. Allanson's enthusiasm, or rather
excitement, seems to have been more than he was
able to bear, as he instantly became delirious with
joy, and always professed that he could remember nothing of their first meeting, save that Mary
remained silent, and spoke not a word, neither good
nor bad. He had no doubt, he said, that his words
and actions both were extravagant; but he had no
conception that they could be anything but respect-
ful; yet, for all that, Mary, who had never uttered

a word, fell a-sobbing and weeping, refusing to be comforted. This melting tenderness the youth had not construed aright; for, on offering some further blandishments, the maid uttered a piercing shriek, sprung up, and ran from him with amazing speed.

At this part of the loch, which, as I said, is well known to many, the shore is overhung by a precipitous cliff, of no great height, but still inaccessible, either from above or below. Save in a great drought, the water comes to within a yard of the bottom of this cliff, and the intermediate space is filled with rough unshapely pieces of rock fallen from above. Along this narrow and rude space, hardly passable by the angler at noon, did Mary bound with the swiftness of a kid, although surrounded with darkness. Her lover, pursuing with all his energy, called out, 'Mary! Mary! my dear Mary, stop and speak with me. I'll conduct you home, or anywhere you please, but do not run from me. Stop, my dearest Mary – stop!'

Mary would not stop; but ran on, till, coming to a little cliff that jutted into the lake, round which there was no passage, and, perceiving that her lover would there overtake her, she uttered another shriek, and plunged into the lake. The loud sound of her fall into the still lake rung in the young man's ears like the knell of death; and if before he was crazed with love, he was now as much so with despair. He saw her floating lightly away from the shore towards the deepest part of the loch; but, in a short time, she began to sink, and gradually disappeared, without uttering a throb or a cry. A good while previous to this, Allanson had flung off his bonnet, shoes, and coat, and plunged in after the treasure of his soul. He swam to the place where she disappeared; but there was neither boil nor gurgle on the water, nor even a bell of departing breath, to mark the place where his beloved had sunk. Being strangely impressed, at that trying moment, either to live or die with her, he tried to dive, in hopes either to bring her up or to die in her arms; and he thought of their being so found on the shore of the lake with a melancholy satisfaction; but by no effort of his could he reach the bottom, nor knew he what distance he was still from it. With an exhausted frame, and a despairing heart, he was obliged again to seek the shore, and, dripping wet as he was, and half naked, he ran to her father's house with the woful tidings. Everything there was quiet. The old shepherd's family, of whom Mary was the youngest, and sole daughter, were all sunk in quiet repose; and oh how the distracted lover wept at the thoughts of wakening them to hear the doleful tidings! But waken them he must; so, going to the little window close by the goodman's bed, he called, in a melancholy tone, 'Andrew! Andrew Burnet, are you waking?'

'Troth, man, I think I be: or, at least, I'm half-an'-half. What hast thou to say to auld Andrew Burnet at this time o' night?'

'Are you waking, I say?'

'Gudewife, am I waking? Because if I be, tell that stravaiger sae. He'll maybe tak' your word for it, for mine he winna tak'.'

'O Andrew, none of your humour tonight; – I bring you tidings the most woful, the most dismal, the most heart-rending, that ever were brought to an honest man's door.'

'To his window, you mean,' cried Andrew, bolting out of bed, and proceeding to the door. 'Gude sauff us, man, come in, whaever you be, an' tell us your tidings face to face; an' then we'll can better judge of the truth of them. If they be in concord wi' your voice, they are melancholy indeed. Have the reavers come, and are our kye driven?'

'Oh, alas! waur than that – a thousand times waur than that! Your daughter – your dear beloved and only daughter, Mary—'

'What of Mary?' cried the gudeman. 'What of Mary?' cried her mother, shuddering and groaning with terror; and at the same time she kindled a light.

The sight of their neighbour, half-naked, and dripping with wet, and madness and despair in his looks, sent a chillness to their hearts, that held them in silence, and they were unable to utter a word, till he went on thus – 'Mary is gone; your darling and mine is lost, and sleeps this night in a watery grave, – and I have been her destroyer.'

'Thou art mad, John Allanson,' said the old man, vehemently, 'raving mad; at least I hope so. Wicked as thou art, thou hadst not a heart to kill my dear child. O yes, you are mad – God be thanked, you are mad. I see it in your looks and whole demeanour. Heaven be praised, you are mad! You *are* mad, but you'll get better again. But what do I say?' continued he, as recollecting himself, – 'We can soon convince our own senses. Wife, lead the way to our daughter's bed.'

With a heart throbbing with terror and dismay, old Jean Linton led the way to Mary's chamber, followed by the two men, who were eagerly gazing, one over each of her shoulders. Mary's little apartment was in the farther end of the long narrow cottage; and as soon as they entered it, they perceived a form lying on the bed, with the bed-clothes drawn over its head; and on the lid of Mary's little chest, that stood at the bed-side, her clothes were lying neatly folded, as they wont to be. Hope seemed to dawn on the faces of the two old people when they beheld this, but the lover's heart sunk still deeper in despair. The father called her name, but the form on the bed returned no answer; however, they all heard distinctly the sobs, as of one weeping. The old man then ventured to pull down the clothes from her face; and, strange to say, there indeed lay Mary Burnet, drowned in tears, yet apparently nowise surprised at the ghastly appearance of the three naked figures. Allanson gasped for breath, for he remained still incredulous. He touched her clothes – he lifted her robes one by one, – and all of them were dry, neat, and clean, and had no appearance of having sunk in the lake.

There can be no doubt that Allanson was confounded by the strange event that had befallen him, and felt like one struggling with a frightful vision, or some energy beyond the power of man to comprehend. Nevertheless, the assurance that Mary was there in life, weeping although she was, put him once more beside himself with joy; and he kneeled at her bedside, beseeching but to kiss her hand. She, however, repulsed him with disdain, uttering these words with great emphasis – 'You are a bad man, John Allanson, and I entreat you to go out of my sight. The sufferings that I have undergone this night have been beyond the power of flesh and blood to endure; and by some cursed agency of yours have these sufferings been brought about. I therefore pray you, in His name, whose law you have transgressed, to depart out of my sight.'

Wholly overcome by conflicting passions, by circumstances so contrary to one another, and so discordant with everything either in the works of Nature or Providence, the young man could do nothing but stand like a rigid statue, with his hands lifted up, and his visage like that of a corpse, until led away by the two old people from their daughter's apartment. They then lighted up a fire to dry him, and began to question him with the most intense curiosity; but they could elicit nothing from him, but the most disjointed exclamations – such as, 'Lord in Heaven, what can be the meaning of this!' And at other times – 'It is all the enchantment of the devil; the evil spirits have got dominion over me!'

Finding they could make nothing of him, they began to form conjectures of their own. Jean affirmed that it had been the Mermaid of the loch that had come to him in Mary's shape, to allure him to his destruction; 'and he had muckle reason to be thankful that he had keepit in some bounds o' decency wi' her, else he wad hae been miserable through life, an' a thousand times waur through eternity.'

But Andrew Burnet, setting his bonnet to one side, and raising his left hand to a level with that, so that he might have full scope to motion and flourish with it, suiting his action to his words, thus began, with a face of sapience never to be excelled: –

'Gudewife, it doth strike me that thou art very wide of the mark. It must have been a spirit of a great deal higher quality than a meer-maiden, who played this extraordinary prank. The meer-maiden is not a spirit, but a beastly sensitive creature, with a malicious spirit within it. Now, what influence could a cauld clatch of a creature like that, wi' a tail like a great saumont-fish, hae owner our bairn, either to make her happy or unhappy? Or where could it borrow her claes, Jean? Tell me that. Na, na, Jean Linton, depend on it, the spirit that courtit wi' poor sinfu' Jock there, has been a fairy; but whether a good ane or an ill ane, it is hard to determine.'

How long Andrew's disquisition might have lasted, will never be known, for it was interrupted by the young man falling into a fit of trembling that was fearful to look at, and threatened soon to terminate his existence. Jean ran for the family cordial, observing, by the way, that 'though he was a wicked person, he was still a fellow-creature, and might live to repent;' and influenced by this spark of genuine humanity, she made him swallow two horn-spoonfuls of strong aquavitae, while Andrew brought out his best Sunday shirt, and put it on him in place of his wet one. Then putting a piece of scarlet thread round each wrist, and taking a strong rowan-tree staff in his hand, he conveyed his trembling and astonished guest home, giving him at parting this sage advice: –

'I'll tell you what it is, Jock Allanson, – ye hae run a near risk o' perdition, an' escaping that for the present, o' losing your right reason. But tak' an auld man's advice – never gang again out by night to beguile ony honest man's daughter, lest a worse thing befall thee.'

Next morning Mary dressed herself more neatly than usual, but there was manifestly a deep melancholy settled on her lovely face, and at times the unbidden tear would start into her eye. She spoke no word, either good or bad, that ever her mother could recollect, that whole morning; but she once or twice observed her daughter gazing at her, as with an intense and melancholy interest. About nine o'clock in the morning, she took a hay-raik over her shoulder, and went down to a meadow at the east end of the loch, to coil a part of her father's hay, her father and brother engaging to join her about noon, when they came from the sheep-fold. As soon as old Andrew came home, his wife and he, as was natural, instantly began to converse on the events of the preceding night; and in the course of their conversation, Andrew said, 'Gudeness be about us, Jean, was not yon an awfu' speech o' our bairn's to young Jock Allanson last night?'

'Ay, it was a downsetter, gudeman, and spoken like a good Christian lass.'

'I'm no sae sure o' that, Jean Linton. My good woman, Jean Linton, I'm no sae sure o' that. Yon speech has gi'en me a great deal o' trouble o' heart, for d'ye ken, an take my life, – ay, an take your life, Jean, – nane o' us can tell whether it was in the Almighty's name, or the devil's, that she discharged her lover.'

'O fy, Andrew, how can ye say sae? How can ye doubt that it was in the Almighty's name?'

'Couldna she have said sae then, and that wad hae put it beyond a' doubt? An' that wad hae been the natural way too; but instead of that, she says, "I pray you, in the name of him whose law you have transgressed, to depart out o' my sight." I confess I'm terrified when I think about yon speech, Jean Linton. Didna she say, too, that "her sufferings had been beyond what flesh an' blood could have endured?" What was she but flesh and blood? Didna that remark infer that she was something mair than a mortal creature? Jean Linton, Jean Linton! what will you say, if it should turn out that our daughter *is* drowned, and that yon was the fairy we had in the house a' the night and this morning?'

'O haud your tongue, Andrew Burnet, an' dinna make my heart cauld within me. We hae aye trusted in the Lord yet, an' he has never forsaken us, nor will he yet gie the wicked power ower us or ours.'

'Ye say very weel, Jean, an' we maun e'en hope for the best,' quoth old Andrew; and away he went, accompanied by his son Alexander, to assist their beloved Mary on the meadow.

No sooner had Andrew set his head over the bents, and come in view of the meadow, than he said to his son, 'I wish Jock Allanson maunna hae been east the loch fishing for geds the day, for I think my Mary has made very little progress in the meadow.'

'She's ower muckle ta'en up about other things this while, to mind her wark,' said Alexander: 'I wadna wonder, father, if that lassie gangs a black gate yet.'

Andrew uttered a long and a deep sigh, that seemed to ruffle the very fountains of life, and, without speaking another word, walked on to the hay field. It was three hours since Mary had left home, and she ought at least to have put up a dozen coils of hay each hour. But, in place of that, she had put up only seven altogether, and the last was unfinished. Her own hay-raik, that had an M and a B neatly cut on the head of it, was leaning on the unfinished coil, and Mary was wanting. Her brother, thinking she had hid herself from them in sport, ran from one coil to another, calling her many bad names, playfully; but, after he had turned them all up, and several deep swathes besides, she was not to be found. Now, it must be remarked, that this young man, who slept in the byre, knew nothing of the events of the foregoing night, the old people and Allanson having mutually engaged to keep them a profound secret. So that, when old Andrew said, 'What in the world can hae come o' the lassie?' his son replied, with a lightsome air, 'Off wi' some o' the lads, to be sure, on some daft errand. Od ye ken little about her; she wad rin through fire an' water to be wi' a handsome young lad. I believe, if the deil himsell war to come to her in the form of a braw, bonny lad, he might persuade her to do ought ever he likit.'

'Whisht, callant, how can ye speak that gate about your only sister? I'm sure, poor lassie, she has never gi'en ane o' us a sair heart in a' her life – till now,' added Andrew, after a long pause; and the young man, perceiving his father looking so serious and thoughtful, dropped his raillery, and they began to work at the hay. Andrew could work none; he looked this way and that way, but in no way could he see Mary approaching: so he put on his coat, and went away home, to pour his sorrows into the bosom of his old wife; and in the meantime, he desired his son to run to all the neighbouring farmhouses and cots, every one, and make inquiries if anybody had seen Mary.

When Andrew went home and informed his wife that their darling was missing, the grief and astonishment of the aged couple knew no bounds. They sat down, and wept together, and declared, over and over, that this act of Providence was too strange for them, and too high to be understood. Jean besought her husband to kneel instantly, and pray urgently to God to restore their child to them; but he declined it, on account of the wrong frame of his mind, for he declared, that his rage against John Allanson was so extreme, as to unfit him for approaching the throne of his Maker. 'But if the profligate refuses to listen to the entreaties of an injured parent,' added he, 'he shall feel the weight of an injured father's arm.'

Andrew went straight away to Inverlawn, though without the least hope of finding young Allanson at home, for he had no doubt that he had seduced his daughter from her duty; but, on reaching the place, to his still farther amazement, he found the young man lying ill of a burning fever, raving incessantly of witches, spirits, and Mary Burnet. To such a height had his frenzy arrived, that when Andrew went there, it required three men to hold him in the bed. Both his parents testified their opinions openly, that their son was bewitched, or possessed of a demon, and the whole family was thrown into the greatest consternation. The good old shepherd, finding enough of grief there already, was obliged to confine his to his own bosom, and return disconsolate to his little family circle, in which there was a woful blank that night.

His son returned also from a fruitless search. No one had seen any traces of his sister, but an old crazy woman, at a place called Oxcleuch, said that she had seen her go by in a grand chariot with young Jock Allanson, toward the Birkhill Path, and by that time they were at the Cross of Dumgree. The young man said he asked her what sort of a chariot it was, as there was never such a thing in that country as a chariot, nor yet a road for one. But she replied, that he was widely mistaken, for that a great number of chariots sometimes passed that way, though never any of them returned. These words appearing to be merely the ravings of superannuation, they were not regarded; but when no other traces of Mary could be found, old Andrew went up to consult this crazy dame once more, but he was not able to bring any such thing to her recollection. She spoke only in parables, which to him were incomprehensible.

Bonny Mary Burnet was lost. She left her father's house at nine o'clock on a Wednesday morning, the 17th of September, neatly dressed in a white jerkin and green bonnet, with her hay-raik over her shoulder; and that was the last sight she was doomed ever to see of her native cottage. She seemed to have had some presentiment of this, as appeared from her demeanour that morning before she left it. Mary Burnet of Kirkstyle was lost, and great was the sensation produced over the whole country by the mysterious event. There was a long ballad extant at one period on the melancholy catastrophe, which was supposed to have been composed by the chaplain of St Mary's, but I have only heard tell of it, without ever hearing it sung or recited. Many of the verses concluded thus: –

But bonny Mary Burnet
We will never see again.

The story soon got abroad, with all its horrid circumstances, and there is little doubt that it was grievously exaggerated. The gossips told of a love-tryst by night, at the side of the loch – of the young profligate's rudeness, which was carried to that degree, that she was obliged to throw herself into the lake, and perish, rather than submit to infamy and sin. In short, there was no obloquy that was not thrown on the survivor, who certainly in some degree deserved it, for, instead of growing better, he grew ten times more wicked than he was before.

In one thing the whole country agreed, that it had been the real Mary Burnet who was drowned in the loch, and that the being which was found in her bed, lying weeping and complaining of suffering, and which vanished the next day, had been a fairy, an evil spirit, or a changeling of some sort, for that it never spoke save once, and that in a mysterious manner; nor did it partake of any food with the rest of the family. Her father and mother knew not what to say or what to think, but they wandered through this weary world like people wandering in a dream.

Everything that belonged to Mary Burnet was kept by her parents as the most sacred relics, and many a tear did her aged mother shed over them. Every article of her dress brought the once comely wearer to mind. The handsome shoes that her feet had shaped, and even the very head of her hay-raik, with an M and B cut upon it, were laid carefully by in the little chest that had once been hers, and served as dear memorials of one that was now no more. Andrew often said, 'That to have lost the darling child of their old age in any way would have been a great trial, but to lose her in the way that they had done, was really mair than human frailty could endure.'

Many a weary day did he walk by the shores of the loch, looking eagerly for some vestige of her garments, and though he trembled at every appearance, yet did he continue to search on. He had a number of small bones collected, that had belonged to lambs and other minor animals, and, haply, some of them to fishes, from a fond supposition that they might once have formed joints of her toes or fingers. These he kept concealed in a little bag, in order, as he said, 'to let the doctors see them.' But no relic, besides these, could he ever discover of his Mary's body.

Young Allanson recovered from his raging fever scarcely in the manner of other men, for he recovered all at once, after a few days' raving and madness. Mary Burnet, it appeared, was by him no more remembered. He grew ten times more wicked than before, and hesitated at no means of accomplishing his unhallowed purposes. His passion for women grew into a mania, that blinded the eyes of his understanding, and hindered him from perceiving the path of moral propriety, or even that of common decency. This total depravity the devout shepherds and cottagers around him regarded as an earthly and eternal curse fixed on him; a mark like that which God put upon Cain, that whosoever knew him might shun him. They detested him, and, both in their families and in the wild, when there was no ear to hear but that of Heaven, they prayed protection from his devices, as if he had been the wicked one; and they all prophesied that he would make a bad end.

One fine day, about the middle of October, when the days begin to get very short, and the nights long and dark, on a Friday morning, the next year but one after Mary Burnet was lost, a memorable day in the fairy annals, John Allanson, younger of Inverlawn, went to a great hiring fair at a village called Moffat in Annandale, in order to hire a housemaid. His character was so notorious, that not one pretty maiden in the district would serve in his father's house; so away he went to the fair at Moffat, to hire the prettiest and loveliest girl he could there find, with the generous intention of seducing her as soon as she came home. This was no suppositious accusation, for he acknowledged his plan to Mr David Welch of Cariferan, who rode down to the market with him, and seemed to boast of it, and dwell on it, with delight. But the maidens of Annandale had a guardian angel in the fair that day, of which neither he nor they were aware.

Allanson looked through the hiring market, and through the hiring market, and at length fixed on one, which indeed was not difficult to do, for there was no such form there for elegance and beauty. She had all the appearance of a lady, but she had the badge of servitude in her bosom, a little rose of Paradise, without the leaves, so that Allanson knew she was to hire. He urged her for some time, with emotions of the wildest delight, and at length meeting with his young companion, Mr David Welch, he pointed her out to him, and asked how she would suit.

Mr Welch answered, that he was in great luck indeed, if he acquired such a mistress as that. '*If?*' said he, – 'I think you need hardly have put an *if* to it. Stop there for a small space, and I will let you see me engage her in five minutes.' Mr Welch stood still and eyed him. He took the beauty aside. She was clothed in green, and as lovely as a new blown rose.

'Are you to hire, pretty maiden?'

'Yes, sir.'

'Will you hire with me?'

'I care not though I do. But if I hire with you, it must be for the long term.'

'Certainly. The longer the better. What are your wages to be?'

'You know, if I hire, I must be paid in kind. I must have the first living creature that I see about Inverlawn to myself.'

'I wish it may be me, then. But what the devil do you know about Inverlawn?'

'I think I *should* know about it.'

'Bless me! I know the face as well as I know my own, and better. But the name has somehow escaped me. Pray, may I ask your name?'

'Hush! hush!' said she solemnly, and holding up her hand at the same time; 'Hush, hush, you had better say nothing about that here.'

'I am in utter amazement!' exclaimed he. 'What is the meaning of this? I conjure you to tell me your name?'

'It is Mary Burnet,' said she, in a soft whisper; and at the same time she let down a green veil over her face.

If Allanson's death-warrant had been announced to him at that moment, it could not have deprived him so completely of sense and motion. His visage changed into that of a corpse, his jaws fell down, and his eyes became glazed, so as apparently to

throw no reflection inwardly. Mr Welch, who had
kept his eye steadily on them all the while, perceived his comrade's dilemma, and went up to
him. 'Allanson? – Mr Allanson? What the deuce
is the matter with you, man?' said he. 'Why, the
girl has bewitched you, and turned you into a
statue!'

Allanson made some sound with his voice, as
if attempting to speak, but his tongue refused its
office, and he only jabbered. Mr Welch, conceiving
that he was seized with some fit, or about to faint,
supported him into the Johnston Arms, and got
him something to drink; but he either could not,
or would not, grant him any explanation. Welch
being, however, resolved to see the maiden in green
once more, persuaded Allanson, after causing him
to drink a good deal, to go out into the hiring-market
again, in search of her. They ranged the market
through and through, but the maiden in green was
gone, and not to be found. She had vanished in
the crowd the moment she divulged her name, and
even though Welch had his eye fixed on her, he
could not discover which way she went. Allanson
appeared to be in a kind of stupor as well as terror,
but when he found that she had left the market,
he screwed his courage to the sticking place once
more, and resolving to have a winsome housemaid

from Annandale, he began again to look out for the top of the market.

He soon found one more beautiful than the last. She was like a sylph, clothed in robes of pure snowy white, with green ribbons. Again he pointed this new flower out to Mr David Welch, who declared that such a perfect model of beauty he had never in his life seen. Allanson, being resolved to have this one at any wages, took her aside, and put the usual question.

'Do you wish to hire, pretty maiden?'

'Yes, sir.'

'Will you hire with me?'

'I care not though I do.'

'What, then, are your wages to be? Come – say? And be reasonable; I am determined not to part with you for a trifle.'

'My wages must be in kind; I work on no other conditions. Pray, how are all the good people about Inverlawn?'

Allanson's breath began to cut, and a chillness to creep through his whole frame, and he answered, with a faltering tongue, –

'I thank you, – much in their ordinary way.'

'And your aged neighbours,' rejoined she, 'are they still alive and well?'

'I – I – I think they are,' said he, panting for

breath. 'But curse me, if I know who I am indebted to for these kind recollections.'

'What,' said she, 'have you so soon forgot Mary Burnet of Kirkstyle?'

Allanson started as if a bullet had gone through his heart. The lovely sylph-like form glided into the crowd, and left the astounded libertine once more standing like a rigid statue, until aroused by his friend, Mr Welch. He tried a third fair one, and got the same answers, and the same name given. Indeed, the first time ever I heard the tale, it bore that he tried *seven*, who all turned out to be Mary Burnets of Kirkstyle; but I think it unlikely that he would try so many, as he must long ere that time have been sensible that he laboured under some power of enchantment. However, when nothing else would do, he helped himself to a good proportion of strong drink. While he was thus engaged, a phenomenon of beauty and grandeur came into the fair, that caught the sole attention of all present. This was a lovely dame, riding in a gilded chariot, with two liverymen before, and two behind, clothed in green and gold; and never sure was there so splendid a meteor seen in a Moffat fair. The word instantly circulated in the market, that this was the Lady Elizabeth Douglas, eldest daughter to the Earl of Morton, who then sojourned at Auchincastle, in the vicinity of Moffat, and which lady at that time was celebrated as a great beauty all over Scotland. She was afterwards Lady Keith; and the mention of this name in the tale, as it were by mere accident, fixes the era of it in the reign of James the Fourth, at the very time that fairies, brownies, and witches, were at the rifest in Scotland.

Every one in the market believed the lady to be the daughter of the Earl of Morton, and when she came to the Johnston Arms, a gentleman in green came out bareheaded, and received her out of the carriage. All the crowd gazed at such unparalleled beauty and grandeur, but none was half so much overcome as Allanson. His heart, being a mere general slave to female charms, was smitten in proportion as this fair dame excelled all others he had ever seen. He had never conceived aught half so lovely either in earth, or heaven, or fairy-land, and his heart, at first sight, burned with an inextinguishable flame of love towards her. But alas, there is reason to fear there was no spark of that refined and virtuous love in him, which is the delight of earth and heaven. It might be more fervent and insufferable, but it wanted the sweet serenity and placid delights of the former. His was not a ray from the paradise above, but a burning spark from the regions below. From thence it arose, and in all its wanderings, thitherward it pointed again.

While he stood in this burning fever of love and admiration, his bosom panting, and his eyes suffused with tears, think of his astonishment, and the astonishment of the countless crowd that looked on, when this brilliant and matchless beauty beckoned him towards her! He could not believe his senses, but looked hither and thither to see how others regarded the affair; but she beckoned him a second time, with such a winning courtesy and smile, that immediately he pulled off his beaver cap and hasted up to her; and without more ado she gave him her arm, and the two walked into the hostel.

Allanson conceived that he was thus distinguished by Lady Elizabeth Douglas, the flower of the land, and so did all the people of the market; and greatly they wondered who the young farmer could be that was thus particularly favoured; for it ought to have been mentioned that he had not one personal acquaintance in the fair save Mr David Welch of Cariferan. But no sooner had she got him into a private room, than she began to inquire kindly of his health and recovery from the severe malady by which he was visited. Allanson thanked her ladyship with all the courtesy he was master of; and being by this time persuaded that she was in love with him, he became as light as if treading on the air. She next inquired after his father and mother. 'Oho!' thinks he to himself, 'poor creature, she is terribly in for it! but her love *shall not* be thrown away upon a backward or ungrateful object.'

He answered her with great politeness, and at length began to talk of her noble father and young Lord William, but she cut him short by asking if he did not recognise her.

'Oh, yes! He knew who her ladyship was, and remembered that he had seen her comely face often before, although he could not recall to his memory the precise time or places of their meeting.'

She asked him for his old neighbours of Kirkstyle, and if they were still in life and health!!

Allanson felt as if his heart were a piece of ice. A chillness spread over his whole frame; he sank back on a seat, and remained motionless; but the beautiful and adorable creature soothed him with kind words, and even with blandishments, till he again gathered courage to speak.

'What!' said he; 'and has it been your own lovely self who has been playing tricks on me this whole day?'

'A first love is not easily extinguished, Mr Allanson,' said she. 'You may guess, from my appearance, that I have been fortunate in life; but, for all that, my first love for you has continued the same, unaltered and unchanged, and you must forgive the little freedoms I used today to try your affections, and the effects my appearance would have on you.'

'It argues something for my good taste, however, that I never pitched on any face for beauty today but your own,' said he. 'But now that we have met once more, we shall not so easily part again. I will devote the rest of my life to you, only let me know the place of your abode.'

'It is hard by,' said she, 'only a very little space from this; and happy, happy, would I be to see you there tonight, were it proper or convenient. But my lord is at present from home, and in a distant country.'

'I should not conceive that any particular hinder-ance to my visit,' said he; 'for, in truth, I account it one of the most fortunate events that has happened to me; and visit you I will, and visit you I shall, this night, – that you may depend upon.'

'But I hope, Mr Allanson, you are not of the same rakish disposition that you were on our first acquaintance? for, if you are, I could not see your face under my roof on any account.'

'Why, the truth is, madam, that the country people reckon me a hundred degrees worse; but I know myself to be, in fact, many thousand degrees better. However, let it suffice, that I have no scruples in visiting my old sweetheart in the absence of her lord, nor are they increased by his great distance from home.'

With great apparent reluctance she at length consented to admit of his visit, and offered to leave one of her gentlemen, whom she could trust, to be his conductor; but this he positively refused. It was his desire, he said, that no eye of man should see him enter or leave her happy dwelling. She said he was a self-willed man, but should have his own way; and after giving him such directions as would infallibly lead him to her mansion, she mounted her chariot and was driven away.

Allanson was uplifted above every sublunary concern. Sinful as the adventure was, he gloried in it, for such adventures were his supreme delight. Seeking out his friend, David Welch, he imparted to him his extraordinary good fortune, but he did not tell him that she was not the Lady Elizabeth Douglas. Welch insisted on accompanying him, but this he would in nowise admit; the other, however, set him on the way, and refused to turn back till he came to the very point of the road next to the lady's splendid mansion; and in spite of all that Allanson could say, Welch remained there till he saw his comrade enter the court-gate, which glowed with lights as innumerable as the stars of the firmament.

'Ah, what a bad girl that Lady Elizabeth Douglas must be for all her beauty,' said Mr Welch to himself. 'But, oh! that I had had that wild fellow's fortune tonight!' David Welch did not think so before that day eight days. Let no man run on in evil, and expect that good will spring out of it.

Allanson had promised to his father and mother to be home on the morning after the fair to breakfast. He came not either that day or the next; and the third day the old man mounted his white pony, and rode away towards Moffat in search of his son. He called at Cariferan on his way, and made inquiries at Mr Welch. The latter manifested some astonishment that the young man had not returned; nevertheless he assured his father of his safety, and desired him to return home; and then with reluctance confessed that the young man was engaged in an amour with the Earl of Morton's beautiful daughter; that he had gone to the castle by appointment, and that he, David Welch, had accompanied him to the gate, and seen him enter, and it was apparent that his reception had been a kind one, since he had tarried so long.

The old man lifted off his bonnet with the one hand, and with the other wiped a tear from his eye, saying, at the same time, 'Then I'll never see him alive again! For several years I have foreseen that women would infallibly be the end of him; and now that he is gone upon his wild adventures in the family of the proud Earl Douglas of Morton, how is it likely that he shall ever escape the fate that in reality he deserves? How inscrutable are the divine decrees! My son was born to the doom that has overtaken him. On the night that he was born, there was a weeping and wailing of women all around our house, and even in the bed where his mother was confined; and as it was a brownie that brought the midwife, no one ever knew who she was, or whence she came. His life has been one of mystery, and his end will be the same.'

Mr Welch, seeing the old man's distress, was persuaded to accompany him on his journey, as the last who had seen his son and seen him enter the castle. On reaching Moffat they found his steed standing at the hostel, whither it had returned in the night of the fair before the company broke up; but the owner had not been heard of since seen in company with Lady Elizabeth Douglas. The old man set out for Auchincastle, taking Mr David Welch along with him; but long ere they reached the place, Mr Welch assured him he would not find his son there, as it was nearly in a different direction that they rode, by appointment, on the evening of the fair. However, to the castle they went, and were admitted to the Earl, who laughed heartily at the old man's tale, and seemed to consider him in a state of derangement. He sent for his daughter Elizabeth, and questioned her concerning her meeting with the son of the old respectable countryman – of her appointment with him on the night of the preceding Friday, and concluded by saying he hoped she had him still in some safe concealment about the castle.

The lady, hearing her father talk thus flippantly, and seeing the serious and dejected looks of the old man towards her, knew not what to say, and asked an explanation. But Mr Welch put a stop to it by declaring to old Allanson that the Lady Elizabeth was not the lady with whom his son made the appointment, for he had seen her, had considered her lineaments very minutely, and would engage to know her again among ten thousand; nor was that the castle to which he had conducted his son, nor anything like it. 'But go with me,' continued he, 'and though I am a stranger in this district, I think I can take you to the very place.'

Away they went again; and Mr Welch traced the road from Moffat, by which young Allanson and he had gone to the appointed place, until, after travelling several miles, they came to a place where a road struck off to the right at an angle. 'Now I know we are right,' said Welch; 'for here we stopped, and your son intreated me to return, which I refused, and accompanied him to yon large tree, and a little way beyond it, from whence I saw him received in at the splendid gate. We shall now be in sight of the mansion in three minutes.'

They passed on to the tree, and a space beyond it; but then Mr Welch lost the use of his speech, as he perceived that there was neither palace nor gate there, but a tremendous gulf, fifty fathoms deep, and a dark stream foaming and boiling below.

'How is this?' said old Allanson. 'There is neither mansion nor habitation of man here!'

Welch's tongue for a long space refused its office, and there he stood like a statue, gazing on the altered and awful scene. 'He only who made the spirits of men,' said he, at last, 'and all the spirits that sojourn in the earth and air, can tell how this is. We are wandering in a world of enchantment, and have been influenced by some agencies above human nature, or without its pale; for here of a certainty did I take leave of your son – and there, in that direction, and apparently either on the verge of that gulf, or the space above it, did I see him received in at the court-gate of a mansion, splendid beyond all conception. How can human comprehension make anything of this?'

They went forward to the verge, Mr Welch leading the way to the very spot on which he saw the gate opened, and there they found marks where a horse had been plunging. Its feet had been over the brink, but it seemed to have recovered itself, and deep, deep down, and far within, lay the mangled corpse of John Allanson; and in this manner, mysterious beyond all example, terminated the career of that wicked and flagitious young man. What a beautiful moral may be extracted from this fairy tale!

But among all these turnings and windings, there is no account given, you will say, of the fate of Mary Burnet; for this last appearance of hers at Moffat seems to have been altogether a phantom or illusion. Gentle and kind reader, I can give you no account of the fate of that maiden; for though the ancient fairy tale proceeds, it seems to me to involve her fate in ten times more mystery than what is previously related, for, if she was not a changeling, or the Queen of the Fairies herself, I can make nothing of her.

The yearly return of the day on which Mary was lost, was observed as a day of mourning by her aged and disconsolate parents, – a day of sorrow, of fasting, and humiliation. Seven years came

and passed away, and the seventh returning day
of fasting and prayer was at hand. On the evening
previous to it, old Andrew was moving along the
sands of the loch, still looking for some relic of
his beloved Mary, when he was aware of a little
shrivelled old man, who came posting towards him.
The creature was not above five spans in height, and
had a face scarcely like that of a human creature; but
he was, nevertheless, civil in his deportment, and
sensible in speech. He bade Andrew a good evening,
and asked him what he was looking for. Andrew
answered, that he was looking for that which he
would never find.

'Pray, what is your name, ancient shepherd?' said
the stranger; 'for methinks I should know something
of you, and perhaps have a commission to you.'

'Alas! why should you ask after my name?' said
Andrew. 'My name is now nothing to any one.'

'Had not you once a beautiful daughter, named
Mary?' said the stranger.

'It is a heart-rending question, man,' said Andrew;
'but certes, I had once a beloved daughter named
Mary.'

'What became of her?' said the stranger.

Andrew shook his head, turned round, and began
to move away; it was a theme that his heart could not
brook. He sauntered along the loch sands, his dim

eye scanning every white pebble as he passed along. There was a hopelessness apparent in his stooping form, his gait, his eye, his features, – in every step that he took there was a hopeless apathy. The dwarf followed him along, and began to expostulate with him. 'Old man, I see you are pining under some real or fancied affliction,' said he. 'But in continuing to do so, you are neither acting according to the dictates of reason nor true religion. What is man that he should fret, or the son of man that he should repine, under the chastening hand of his Maker?'

'I am far frae justifying mysell,' returned Andrew, surveying his shrivelled monitor with some degree of astonishment. 'But there are some feelings that neither reason nor religion can o'ermaster; and there are some that a parent may cherish without sin.'

'I deny the position,' said the stranger, 'taken either absolutely or in relative degree. All repining under the Supreme decree is leavened with unrighteousness. But, subtleties aside, I ask you, as I did before, What became of your daughter?'

'Ask the Father of her spirit, and the framer of her body,' said Andrew, solemnly; 'ask Him into whose hands I committed her from childhood. He alone knows what became of her, but *I do not*.'

'How long is it since you lost her?'

'It is seven years tomorrow.'

'Ay! you remember the time well. And are you mourning for her all this while?'

'Yes; and I will go down to the grave mourning for my only daughter, the child of my age, and of all my affection. O, thou unearthly-looking monitor, knowest thou aught of my darling child? for if thou dost, thou wilt know, that she was not like other women. There was a simplicity, a purity, and a sublimity about my lovely Mary, that was hardly consistent with our frail nature.'

'Wouldst thou like to see her again?' said the dwarf, snappishly.

Andrew turned round his whole frame, shaking as with a palsy, and gazed on the audacious shrimp. 'See her again, creature!' cried he vehemently – 'Would I like to see her again, say'st thou?'

'I said so,' said the dwarf, 'and I say farther, Dost thou know this token? Look and see if thou dost.'

Andrew took the token, and looked at it, then at the shrivelled stranger, and then at the token again; and at length he burst into tears, and wept aloud; but they were tears of joy, and his weeping seemed to have some breathings of laughter intermingled in it. And still as he kissed and kissed the token, he brayed out in broken and convulsive

sentences, – 'Yes, auld body, I *do* know it! – I *do*
know it! – I *do* know it! It is indeed the same
golden Edward, with three holes in it, with which
I presented my Mary on her birth day, in her
eighteenth year, to buy her a new suit for the
holidays. But when she took it, she said – ay, I
mind weel what my bonny woman said, – "It is
sae bonny and sae kenspeckle," said she, "that I
think I'll keep it for the sake of the giver." O, dear,
dear! and blessed little creature, tell me how she is,
and where she is? Is she living, or is she dead? Is she
in earth or in heaven? for I ken weel she is in ane
of them.'

'She is living, and in good health,' said the dwarf;
'and better, and brawer, and happier, and lovelier
than ever; and if you make haste, you will see her and
her family at Moffat tomorrow afternoon. They are
to pass there on a journey, but it is an express one,
and I am sent to you with that token, to inform you
of the circumstance, that you may have it in your
power to see and embrace your beloved daughter
once before you die.'

'And am I to meet my Mary at Moffat? Come
away, little, dear, welcome body, thou blessed of
heaven, come away, and taste of an auld shepherd's
best cheer, and I'll gang foot for foot with you to
Moffat, and my auld wife shall gang foot for foot

with us too. I tell you, little, blessed, and welcome crile, come along with me.'

'I may not tarry to enter your house, or taste of your cheer, good shepherd,' said the being. 'May plenty still be within your walls, and a thankful heart to enjoy it. But my directions are neither to taste meat nor drink in this country, but to haste back to her that sent me. Go – haste, and make ready, for you have no time to lose.'

'At what time will she be there?' cried Andrew, flinging the plaid from him, to run home with the tidings.

'Precisely when the shadow of the Holy Cross falls due east,' cried the dwarf; and turning round, he hasted on his way.

When old Jean Linton saw her husband coming hobbling and running home without his plaid, and having his doublet flying wide open, she had no doubt that he had lost his wits; and, full of anxiety, she met him at the side of the kail-yard. 'Gudeness preserve us a' in our right senses, Andrew Burnet, what's the matter wi' you?'

'Stand out o' my gate, wife, for, d'ye see, I'm rather in a haste.'

'I see that, indeed, gudeman; but stand still, an' tell me what has putten you *in* sic a haste. Ir ye drunken or ir ye dementit?'

'Na, na; but I'm gaun awa till Moffat.'

'O, gudeness pity the poor auld body! How can ye gang to Moffat, man? Or what have ye to do at Moffat? Dinna ye mind that the morn is the day o' our solemnity?'

'Haud out o' my gate, auld wife, an' dinna speak o' solemnities to me. I'll keep it at Moffat the morn. – Ay, gudewife, an' ye shall keep it at Moffat, too. What d'ye think o' that, woman? Too-whoo, ye dinna ken the mettle that's in an auld body till it be tried.'

'Andrew – Andrew Burnet!'

'Get away wi' your frightened looks, woman; an' haste ye, gang an' fling me out my Sabbath-day claes. An', Jean Linton, my woman, d'ye hear, gang an' pit on your bridal gown, and your silk hood, for ye maun be at Moffat the morn too; an' it is mair nor time we were away. Dinna look sae bumbazed, woman, till I tell ye, that our ain Mary is to meet us at Moffat the morn.'

'O, Andrew! dinna sport wi' the last feelings of an auld forsaken heart.'

'Gude forbid, my auld wife, that I ever sported wi' feeling o' yours,' cried Andrew, clasping her in his arms, and bursting into tears; 'they are a' as sacred to me as breathings frae the Throne o' Grace. But it is true that I tell ye; our dear bairn is to meet us at Moffat the morn, wi' a son in every hand; an' we maun e'en gang an' see her aince again, an' kiss her an' bless her afore we dee.'

The tears now rushed from the old woman's eyes like fountains, and dropped from her sorrow-worn cheeks to the earth, and then, as with a spontaneous movement, she threw her skirt over her head, kneeled down at her husband's feet, and poured out her soul in thanksgiving to her Maker. She then rose up quite deprived of her senses through joy, and ran crouching away on the road towards Moffat, as if hasting beyond her power to be at it. But Andrew brought her back; and they prepared themselves for their journey.

Kirkstyle being twenty miles from Moffat, they set out on the afternoon of Tuesday, the 16th of September; slept that night at a place called Turnberry Sheil, and were in Moffat next day by noon. Wearisome was the remainder of the day to that aged couple; they wandered about conjecturing by what road their daughter would come, and how she would come attended. 'I have made up my mind on baith these matters,' said Andrew; 'at first I thought it was likely that she would come out o' the east, because a' our blessings come frae that airt; but finding now that that would be o'er near to the very road we hae come oursells, I now take it for granted she'll come frae the south; an' I just think I see her leading a bonny boy in every hand, an' a servant lass carrying a bit bundle ahint her.'

The two now walked out on all the southern roads, in hopes to meet their Mary, but always returned to watch the shadow of the Holy Cross; and, by the time it fell due east, they could do nothing but stand in the middle of the street, and look round them in all directions. At length, about half a mile out on the Dumfries road, they perceived a poor beggar woman approaching with two children following close to her, and another beggar a good way behind. Their eyes were instantly riveted on these objects; for Andrew thought he perceived his friend the dwarf in the one that was behind; and now all other earthly objects were to them nothing, save these approaching beggars. At that moment a gilded chariot entered the village from the south, and drove by them at full speed, having two livery men before, and two behind, clothed in green and gold. 'Ach-wow! the vanity of worldly grandeur!' said Andrew, as the splendid vehicle went thundering by; but neither he nor his wife deigned to look at it farther, their whole attention being fixed on the group of beggars. 'Ay, it is just my woman,' said Andrew, 'it is just hersell; I ken her gang yet, sair pressed down wi' poortith although she be. But I dinna care how poor she be, for baith her an' hers sall be welcome to my fireside as lang as I hae ane.'

While their eyes were thus strained, and their hearts melting with tenderness and pity, Andrew felt something embracing his knees, and, on looking down, there was his Mary, blooming in splendour and beauty, kneeling at his feet. Andrew uttered a loud hysterical scream of joy, and clasped her to his bosom; and old Jean Linton stood trembling, with her arms spread, but durst not close them on so splendid a creature, till her daughter first enfolded her in a fond embrace, and then she hung upon her and wept. It was a wonderful event – a restoration without a parallel. They indeed beheld their Mary, their long-lost darling; they held her in their embraces, believed in her identity, and were satisfied. Satisfied, did I say? They were happy beyond the lot of mortals. She had just alighted from her chariot; and, perceiving her aged parents standing together, she ran and kneeled at their feet. They now retired into the hostel, where Mary presented her two sons to her father and mother. They spent the evening in every social endearment; and Mary loaded the good old couple with rich presents, watched over them till midnight, when they both fell into a deep and happy sleep, and then she remounted her chariot, and was driven away. If she was any more seen in Scotland, I never heard of it; but her parents rejoiced in the thoughts of her happiness till the day of their death.

Kilmeny

BONNY KILMENY gaed up the glen;
But it wasna to meet Duneira's men,
Nor the rosy monk of the isle to see,
For Kilmeny was pure as pure could be.
It was only to hear the Yorlin sing   yellow-hammer
And pu' the cress-flower round the spring;
The scarlet hypp and the hindberrye,   wild raspberry
And the nut that hang frae the hazel tree;
For Kilmeny was pure as pure
   could be.
But lang may her minny look o'er the wa',   mother
And lang may she seeki' the green-wood   thicket
   shaw;
Lang the laird of Duneira blame,
And lang, lang greet or Kilmeny come hame!   weep; before

   When many a day had come
      and fled,
When grief grew calm, and hope
   was dead,
When mess for Kilmeny's soul had
   been sung,

When the bedes-man had prayed, and the
    deadbell rung,
Late, late in a gloamin when all was still,   twilight
When the fringe was red on the
    westlin hill,
The wood was sere, the moon i' the wane,
The reek o' the cot hung over the plain,   smoke; cottage
Like a little wee cloud in the world its lane;   on its own
When the ingle lowed with an eiry leme,   hearth blazed; gleam
Late, late in the gloamin Kilmeny
    came hame!

   'Kilmeny, Kilmeny, where have
     you been?
Lang hae we sought baith holt and den;   wooded hill; ravine
By linn, by ford, and green-wood tree,   waterfall pool
Yet you are halesome and fair to see.
Where gat you that joup o' the lilly scheen?   skirt
That bonny snood of the birk sae green?   girl's hairband; birch
And these roses, the fairest that ever
    were seen?
Kilmeny, Kilmeny, where have you been?'

   Kilmeny looked up with a lovely grace,
But nae smile was seen on Kilmeny's face;
As still was her look, and as still
    was her ee,

As the stillness that lay on the emerant lea,   emerald pasture
Or the mist that sleeps on a waveless sea.
For Kilmeny had been she knew
   not where,
And Kilmeny had seen what she could
   not declare,
Kilmeny had been where the cock
   never crew,
Where the rain never fell, and the wind
   never blew,
But it seemed as the harp of the sky
   had rung,
And the airs of heaven played round
   her tongue,
When she spake of the lovely forms she
   had seen,
And a land where sin had never been,
A land of love, and a land of light,
Withouten sun, or moon, or night:
Where the river swa'd a living stream,   swelled
And the light a pure celestial beam:
The land of vision it would seem,
A still, an everlasting dream.

   In yon green-wood there is a waik,   walk
And in that waik there is a wene,   dwelling
   And in that wene there is a maike,   mate/companion

That neither has flesh, blood, nor
　　bane;
　　　And down in yon green-wood he
　　　　walks his lane.

　　In that green wene Kilmeny lay,
Her bosom happed wi' the flowerits gay;　　covered
But the air was soft and the silence deep,
And bonny Kilmeny fell sound asleep.
She kend nae mair, nor opened her ee,
Till waked by the hymns of a far
　　countrye.

　　She 'wakened on couch of the silk
　　　sae slim,
All striped wi' the bars of the rainbow's
　　rim;
And lovely beings round were rife,
Who erst had travelled mortal life;　　once
And aye they smiled, and 'gan to speer,　　began to ask
'What spirit has brought this mortal
　　here?' –

　　'Lang have I journeyed the world
　　　wide,'
A meek and reverend fere replied;　　comrade/companion

'Baith night and day I have watched the
    fair,
Eident a thousand years and mair.   Diligent
Yes, I have watched o'er ilk degree,   each
Wherever blooms femenitye;
But sinless virgin, free of stain
In mind and body, fand I nane.
Never, since the banquet of time,
Found I a virgin in her prime,
Till late this bonny maiden I saw
As spotless as the morning snaw:
Full twenty years she has lived as free
As the spirits that sojourn this
    countrye.
I have brought her away frae the
    snares of men,
That sin or death she never may ken.' –

    They clasped her waiste and her
        hands sae fair,
They kissed her cheek, and they kemed   combed
    her hair,
And round came many a blooming fere,   companion
Saying, 'Bonny Kilmeny, ye're welcome
    here!
Women are freed of the littand scorn: blush-making
O, blessed be the day Kilmeny was born!

Now shall the land of the spirits see,
Now shall it ken what a woman may be!
Many a lang year in sorrow and pain,
Many a lang year through the world
   we've gane,
Commissioned to watch fair womankind,
For it's they who nurice th'immortal
   mind.
We have watched their steps as the
   dawning shone,
And deep in the green-wood walks alone;
By lilly bower and silken bed,
The viewless tears have o'er them shed,   invisible
Have soothed their ardent minds to sleep,
Or left the couch of love to weep.
We have seen! we have seen! but the time
   must come,
And the angels will weep at the day
   of doom!

    'O, would the fairest of mortal kind
Aye keep the holy truths in mind,
That kindred spirits their motions see,
Who watch their ways with anxious ee,
And grieve for the guilt of humanitye!
O, sweet to Heaven the maiden's prayer,
And the sigh that heaves a bosom sae fair!

And dear to Heaven the words of truth,

And the praise of virtue frae beauty's
  mouth!

And dear to the viewless forms of air,

The minds that kyth as the body fair!   appear

'O, bonny Kilmeny! free frae stain,

If ever you seek the world again,

That world of sin, of sorrow and fear,

O, tell of the joys that are waiting here;

And tell of the signs you shall shortly see,

Of the times that are now, and the times
  that shall be.' –

They lifted Kilmeny, they led
    her away,

And she walked in the light of a
    sunless day:

The sky was a dome of crystal bright,

The fountain of vision, and fountain of
  light:

The emerald fields were of dazzling glow,

And the flowers of everlasting blow.

Then deep in the stream her body
  they laid,

That her youth and beauty never
  might fade;

And they smiled on heaven, when they
    saw her lie
In the stream of life that wandered bye.
And she heard a song, she heard it sung,
She kend not where; but sae sweetly it rung,   knew
It fell on her ear like a dream of
    the morn:
'O! blest be the day Kilmeny was born!
Now shall the land of the spirits see,
Now shall it ken what a woman may be!
The sun that shines on the world
    sae bright,
A borrowed gleid frae the fountain of light;   spark
And the moon that sleeks the sky sae dun,   dusky
Like a gouden bow, or a beamless sun,
Shall wear away, and be seen nae mair,
And the angels shall miss them travelling
    the air.
But lang, lang after baith night and day,
When the sun and the world have elyed away;   slipped slowly
When the sinner has gane to his
    waesome doom,
Kilmeny shall smile in eternal bloom!' –

    They bore her away she wist not how,   knew
For she felt not arm nor rest
    below;

But so swift they wained her through the
   light, carried
'Twas like the motion of sound or sight;
They seemed to split the gales of air,
And yet nor gale nor breeze was there.
Unnumbered groves below them grew,
They came, they past, and backward flew,
Like floods of blossoms gliding on,
In moment seen, in moment gone.
O, never vales to mortal view
Appeared like those o'er which they flew!
That land to human spirits given,
The lowermost vales of the storied heaven;
From thence they can view the
   world below,
And heaven's blue gates with sapphires
   glow,
More glory yet unmeet to know.   unfitting

    They bore her far to a mountain
       green,
To see what mortal never had seen,
And they seated her high on a
   purple sward,
And bade her heed what she saw
   and heard,
And note the changes the spirits wrought,

For now she lived in the land of thought.
She looked, and she saw nor sun nor skies,
But a crystal dome of a thousand dies.
She looked, and she saw nae land aright,
But an endless whirl of glory and light.
And radiant beings went and came
Far swifter than wind, or the linked flame.
She hid her een frae the dazzling view,
She looked again and the scene was new.

She saw a sun on a summer sky,
And clouds of amber sailing bye,
A lovely land beneath her lay,   (Scotland)
And that land had glens and mountains
    gray;
And that land had vallies and hoary piles,
And marled seas, and a thousand isles;
Its fields were speckled, its forests green,
And its lakes were all of the dazzling
    sheen,
Like magic mirrors, where slumbering lay
The sun and the sky and the cloudlet gray;
Which heaved and trembled and
    gently swung,
On every shore they seemed to be hung
For there they were seen on their
    downward plain

A thousand times and a thousand again;
In winding lake and placid firth,
Little peaceful heavens in the bosom
    of earth.

Kilmeny sighed and seemed to grieve,
For she found her heart to that land
    did cleave,
She saw the corn wave on the vale,
She saw the deer run down the dale;
She saw the plaid and the broad
    claymore,
And the brows that the badge of
    freedom bore;
And she thought she had seen the
    land before.

She saw a lady sit on a throne,
The fairest that ever the sun shone on!
A lion licked her hand of milk,
And she held him in a leish of silk;
And a leifu' maiden stood at her knee,
With a silver wand and melting ee;
Her sovereign shield till love stole in,
And poisoned all the fount within.

Then a gruff untoward bedeman came,   man of prayer
And hundit the lion on his dame:

And the guardian maid wi' the dauntless
 ee,
She dropped a tear, and left her knee;
And she saw till the queen frae the
 lion fled,
Till the bonniest flower of the world
 lay dead.
A coffin was set on a distant plain,
And she saw the red blood fall like rain:
Then bonny Kilmeny's heart grew sair,
And she turned away, and could look
 nae mair.

 Then the gruff grim carle girned   fellow, complained
  amain,
And they trampled him down, but he
 rose again;
And he baited the lion to deeds of weir,   war
Till he lapped the blood to the kingdom
 dear;
And weening his head was danger-preef,   imagining
When crowned with the rose and
 clover leaf,
He gowled at the carle, and chased him   bellowed
 away
To feed wi' the deer on the mountain
 gray.

He gowled at the carle, and he gecked at   mocked/gawped
   heaven,
But his mark was set, and his arles given.   deserts
Kilmeny a while hereen withdrew;
She looked again, and the scene was new.

   She saw below her fair unfurled
One half of all the glowing world,
Where oceans rolled, and rivers ran,
To bound the aims of sinful man.
She saw a people, fierce and fell,   cruel
Burst frae their bounds like fiends
   of hell;
There lilies grew, and the eagle flew,
And she herked on her ravening crew,   whispered
Till the cities and towers were wrapt
   in a blaze,
And the thunder it roared o'er the lands
   and the seas.
The widows they wailed, and the red
   blood ran,
And she threatened an end to the
   race of man:
She never lened, nor stood in awe,   rested
Till claught by the lion's deadly paw.
Oh! then the eagles winked for life,   struggled
And brainzelled up a mortal strife;   erupted

But flew she north, or flew she south,
She met wi' the gowl of the lion's mouth.

With a mooted wing and waefu'   moulted
    maen,   demeanour
The eagle sought her eiry again;
But lang may she cour in her bloody nest,
And lang, lang sleek her wounded breast,
Before she sey another flight, try
To play wi' the norland lion's might.

But to sing the sights Kilmeny saw,
So far surpassing nature's law,
The singer's voice wad sink away,
And the string of his harp wad cease to
    play.
But she saw till the sorrows of man
    were bye,
And all was love and harmony,
Till the stars of heaven fell calmly away,
Like the flakes of snaw on a winter day.

Then Kilmeny begged again to see
The friends she had left in her own
    country,
To tell of the place where she had been,

And the glories that lay in the
   land unseen,
To warn the living maidens fair,
The loved of Heaven, the spirits' care,
That all whose minds unmeled remain   innocent
Shall bloom in beauty when time is gane.

   With distant music, soft and deep,
They lulled Kilmeny sound asleep;
And when she awakened, she lay her lane,
All happed with flowers in the greenwood
   wene.   dwelling
When seven lang years had come and fled;
When grief was calm, and hope was dead;
When scarce was remembered Kilmeny's
   name,
Late, late in a gloamin Kilmeny
   came hame!
And O, her beauty was fair to see,
But still and stedfast was her ee!
Such beauty bard may never declare,
For there was no pride nor passion there;
And the soft desire of maiden seen
In that mild face could never be seen.
Her seymar was the lilly flower,   loose upper
And her cheek the moss-rose in the   garment (shawl)
   shower;

And her voice like the distant melodye,
That floats along the twilight sea.
But she loved to raike the lanely glen,   roam
And keeped afar frae the haunts of men;
Her holy hymns unheard to sing,
To suck the flowers, and drink the spring.
But wherever her peaceful form appeared,
The wild beasts of the hill were cheered,
The wolf played blythly round the field,
The lordly byson lowed and kneeled;
The dun deer wooed with manner bland,
And cowered aneath her lilly hand.
And when at even the woodlands rung,
When hymns of other worlds she sung,
In ecstacy of sweet devotion,
O, then the glen was all in motion.
The wild beasts of the forest came,
Broke from their bughts and faulds the   enclosures
    tame,
And goved around, charmed and amazed;   gazed
Even the dull cattle crooned and gazed,
And murmured and looked with
    anxious pain
For something the mystery to explain.
The buzzard came with the throstle-cock;
The corby left her houf in the rock;   raven; haunt
The blackbird alang wi' the eagle flew;

The hind came tripping o'er the dew,

The wolf and the kid their raike began,   journey

And the tod, and the lamb, and the leveret   fox; hare
    ran;

The hawk and the hern attour them hung,   heron; around

And the merl and the mavis forhooyed their   blackbird; thrush; abandoned
    young;

And all in a peaceful ring were hurled:

It was like an eve in a sinless world!

     When a month and a day had come
       and gane,

Kilmeny sought the greenwood wene;

There laid her down on the leaves
    sae green,

And Kilmeny on earth was nevermair seen.

But O, the words that fell from
    her mouth,

Were words of wonder, and words
    of truth!

But all the land were in fear and dread,

For they kendna whether she was living or   knew not
    dead.

It wasna her hame, and she couldna
    remain;

She left this world of sorrow and pain,

And returned to the land of thought again.